FALCONS OF NARRABEDLA

FALCONS OF NARRABEDLA

by Marion Zimmer Bradley

Originally published in Other Worlds, May 1957

CONTENTS

VOLTAGE FROM NOWHERE!

Somewhere on the crags above us I heard a big bird scream. I turned to Andy, knee-deep in the icy stream beside me. "There's your eagle. Probably smells that cougar I shot yesterday." I started to reel in my line, knowing what my brother's next move would be. "Get the camera, and we'll try for a picture."

We crouched together in the underbrush, watching, as the big bird of prey wheeled down in a slow spiral toward the dead cougar. Andy was trembling with excitement, the camera poised against his chest, his eyes glued in the image-finder. "Golly—" he whispered, almost prayerfully, "six foot wing spread—maybe more—"

The bird screamed again, warily, head cocked into the wind. We were to leeward; the scent of the carrion masked our enemy smell from him. The eagle failed to scent or to see us, swooping down and dropping on the cougar's head. Andy's camera clicked twice. The eagle thrust in its beak—

A red-hot wire flared in my brain. The bird—the bird—I leaped out of cover, running swiftly across the ten-foot clearing that separated us from the attacking eagle, my hand tugging automatically at the hunting knife in my belt. Andy's shout of surprised anger was a faraway noise in my ears as the eagle started away with flapping, angry wings—then, in fury, swept down at me, pinions beating around my head. I heard and felt the wicked beak dart in, and thrust blindly upward with the knife, ripped, slashing, hearing the bird's scream of pain and the flapping of wide wings. A red haze spun around me—

Then the screaming eagle was gone and Andy's angry grip was on my shoulder, shaking me roughly. His voice, furious and frightened, was hardly recognizable. "Mike! Mike, you darned idiot, are you all right? You must be crazy!"

I blinked, rubbing my hand across my eyes. The hand came away wet. I was standing in the clearing, the knife in my hand red with blood. Bird blood. I heard myself ask, stupidly "What happened?"

My brother's face came clear out of the thickness in my mind, scowling wrathfully. "You tell *me* what happened! Mike, what in the devil were you thinking about? You told me yourself that an eagle will attack a man if he's bothered. I had him square in the camera when you jumped out of there like a bat out of a belfry and went for the eagle with your knife! You must be clean crazy!"

I let the knife drop out of my hand. "Yeah—" I said heavily, "Yeah, I guess I spoiled your picture, Andy. I'm sorry—I didn't—" my voice trailed off, helpless. The boy's hand was still on my shoulder; he let it drop and knelt in the grass, groping there for his camera. "That's all right, Mike," he said in a dead voice, "you scared the daylights out of me, that's all." He stood up swiftly, looking straight into my face. "Darn it, Mike, you've been acting crazy for a week! I don't mind the blamed camera, but when you start going for eagles with your bare hands—" abruptly he flung the camera away, turned and began to run down the slope in the direction of the cabin.

I took a step to follow, then stopped, bending to retrieve the broken pieces of Andy's cherished camera. The kid must have hit the eagle with it. Lucky thing for me; an eagle can be a mean bird. But why, why in the living hell had I done a thing like that? I'd warned Andy time and time again to stay clear of the big birds. Now that the urgency of action had deserted me, I felt stupid and a little lightheaded. I didn't wonder Andy thought I was crazy. I thought so myself more than half the time. I stowed the broken camera in my tackle box, mentally promising Andy a better one; hunted up the abandoned lines and poles, carefully stowed them, cleaned our day's catch. It was dark before I started for the cabin; I could hear the hum of the electric dynamo I'd rigged up and see the electric light across the dusk of the Sierras. A smell of bacon greeted me as I crossed into the glare of the unshielded bulb. Andy was standing at the cookstove, his back stubbornly to me. He did not turn.

"Andy—" I said.

"It's okay, Mike. Sit down and eat your supper. I didn't wait for the fish."

"Andy—I'll get you another camera—"

"I said, it's okay. Now, damn it, eat."

He didn't speak again for a long time; but as I stretched back for a second mug of coffee, he got up and began to walk around the room, restlessly. "Mike—" he said entreatingly, "you came here for a rest! Why can't you lay off your everlasting work for a while and relax?" He looked disgustedly over his shoulder at the work table where the light spilled over a confused litter of wires and magnets and coils. "You've turned this place into a branch office of General Electric!"

"I can't stop now!" I said violently. "I'm on the track of something—and if I stop I'll never find it!"

"Must be real important," Andy said sourly, "if it makes you act like bughouse bait."

I shrugged without answering. We'd been over that before. I'd known it when they threw me out of the government lab, just after the big blowup. I thought, an-grily. I'm heading for another one, but I don't care.

"Sit down, Andy," I told him. "You don't know what happened down there. Now that the war's over, it's no military secret, and I'll tell you what happened."

I paused, swallowing down the coffee, not knowing that it scalded my mouth. "That is—I will if I can."

Six months before they settled the war in Korea, I was working in a government radio lab, on some new communications equipment. Since I never finished it, there's no point in going into details; it's enough to say it would have made radar as obsolete as the stagecoach. I'd built a special supersonic condenser, and had had trouble with a set of magnetic coils that wouldn't wind properly. When the thing blew up I hadn't had any sleep for three nights, but that wasn't the reason. I was normal then; just another communications man, intent on radio and this new equipment and without any of the crazy impractical notions that had lost me my job later. They called it overwork, but I knew they thought the explosion had disturbed my brain. I didn't blame them. I would have liked to think so. It started one day in the lab with a shadow on the sun and an elusive short circuit that gave me shock after shock until I was jittery. By the time I had it fixed, the oscillator had gone out of control. I got a series of low-frequency waves that were like nothing I'd ever seen before. Then there was something like a voice speaking out of a very old, jerry-built amateur radio set. Except that there wasn't a receiver in the lab, and no one else had heard it. I wasn't sure myself, because right then every instrument in the place went haywire and five minutes later, part of the ceiling hit the floor and the floor went up through the roof. They found me, they say, lying half-crushed under a beam, and I woke up eighteen hours later in a hospital with four cracked ribs, and a feeling as if I'd had a lot of voltage poured into me. It went in the report that I'd been struck by lightning.

It took me a long time to get well. The ribs healed fast—faster than the doctor liked. I didn't mind the hospital part, except that I couldn't walk without shaking, or light a cigarette without burning myself, for months. The thing I minded was what I remembered *before* I woke up. Delirium; that was what they told me. But the kind and *type* of scars on my body didn't ring true. Electricity—even freak lightning— doesn't make that kind of burns. And my corner of the world doesn't make a habit of branding people.

But before I could show the scars to anybody outside the hospital, they were gone. Not healed; just gone. I remembered the look on the medic's face when I showed him the place where the scars had been. He didn't think I was crazy; he thought he was. I knew the lab hadn't been struck by lightning. The Major knew it too; I found that out the day I reported back to work. All the time we talked, his big pen moved in stubby circles across the page of his logbook, and he talked without raising his head to look at me. "I know all that, Kenscott. No electrical storms reported in the vicinity; no radio disturbance within a thousand miles. But—" his jaw grew stubborn, "the lab was wrecked and you were hurt. We've got to have something for the record."

I could understand all that. What I resented was the way they treated me after I went back to work. They transferred me to another division and another line of work. They turned down my request to follow up those nontypical waves. My private notes were ripped out of my notebook while I was at lunch and I never saw them again. And as soon as they could, they shipped me to Fairbanks, Alaska, and that was the end of that.

The Major told me all I needed to know, the day before I took the plane to Alaska. His scowl said more than his words, and they said plenty. "I'd let it alone, Kenscott. No sense stirring up more trouble. We can't bother with side alleys, anyhow. Next time you monkey with it, you might get your head blown off, not just a dose of stray voltage out of the blue. We've done everything but stand on our heads trying to find out where that spare energy came from—and where it went. But we've marked that whole line of research closed, Kenscott. If I were you, I'd keep my mouth shut about it."

"It wasn't a message from Mars," I suggested unsmiling, and he didn't think that was funny either. But there was relief on his face as I left the office and went to clean out my drawer.

I got along all right in Alaska, for a while. But I wasn't the same. The armistice had hardly been signed when they sent me back to the States with a recommendation of overwork. I tried to explain it to Andy. "They said I needed a rest. Maybe so. The shock did something funny to me ... tore me open ... like the electric shock treatments they give catatonic patients. I know a lot of things I never learned. Ordinary radio work doesn't mean anything to me any more. It doesn't make sense. When people out west were talking about flying saucers or whatever they were—and when they talked about weather disturbances after the atomic tests, things did make sense for a while. And when we came down here—" I paused, trying to fit confused impressions together. He wasn't going to believe me, anyhow, but I wanted him to. A tree slapped against the cabin window; I jumped. "It started up again the day we came up in the mountains. Energy out of nowhere, following me around. It can't knock me out. Have you noticed I let you turn the lights on and off? The day we came up, I shorted my electric razor and blew out five fuses trying to change one."

"Yeah, I remember, you had to drive to town for them—" My brother's eyes watched me, uneasy. "Mike, you're kidding—"

"I wish I were," I said. "That energy just drains into me, and nothing happens. I'm immune." I shrugged, rose and walked across to the radio I'd put in here, so carefully, before the war. I picked up the disconnected plug; thrust it into the socket. I snapped the dial on. "I'll show you," I told him.

The panel flashed and darkened; confused static came cracking from the speaker, erratic. I took my hand away.

"Turn it up—" Andy said uneasily.

My hand twiddled the dial. "It's already up." "Try another station;" the kid insisted stubbornly. I pushed all the buttons in succession; the static crackled and buzzed, the panel light flickered on and off in little cryptic flashes. I sighed. "And reception was perfect at noon," I told him, "You were listening to the news." I took my hand away again. "I don't want to blow the thing up."

Andy came over and switched the button back on. The little panel light glowed steadily, and the mellow voice of Milton Cross filled the room ...

"now conduct the Boston Philharmonic Orchestra in the Fifth or 'Fate' symphony of Ludwig von Beethoven ..." the noise of mixed applause, and then the majestic chords of the symphony, thundering through the rooms of the cabin.

"Ta-da-da-dumm——Ta-da-da-DUMM!"

My brother stared at me as racing woodwinds caught up with the brasses. There was nothing wrong with the radio. "Mike. What did you do to it?" "I wish I knew," I told him. Reaching, I touched the volume button again.

Beethoven died in a muttering static like a thousand drums.

I swore and Andy sucked in his breath between his teeth, edging warily backward. He touched the dials again; once more the smoothness of the "Fate" symphony rolled out and swallowed us. I shivered.

"You'd better let it alone!" Andy said shakily. The kid turned in early, but I stayed in the main room, smoking restlessly and wishing I could get a drink without driving eighty miles over bad mountain roads. Neither of us had thought to turn off the radio; it was moaning out some interminable throbbing jazz. I turned over my notes, restlessly, not really seeing them. Once Andy's voice came sleepily from the alcove.

"Going to read all night, Mike?" "If I feel like it," I said tersely and began walking up and down again.

"Michael! For the luvvagod stop it and let me get some sleep!" Andy exploded, and I sank down in the chair again. "Sorry, Andy."

Where had the intangible part of me been, those eighteen hours when I first lay crushed under a fallen beam, then under morphine in the hospital? Where had those scars come from? More important, what had made a radio lab blow up in the first place? Electricity sets fires; it shocks men into insensibility or death. It doesn't explode. Radio waves are in themselves harmless. Most important of all, what maniac freak of lightning was I carrying in my body that made me immune to electrical current? I hadn't told Andy about the time I'd deliberately grounded the electric dynamo in the cellar and taken the whole voltage in my body. I was still alive. It would have been a hell of a way to commit suicide—but I hadn't.

I swore, slamming down the window. I was going to bed. Andy was right. Either I was crazy or there was something wrong; in any case, sitting here wouldn't help. If it didn't let up, I'd take the first train home and see a good electrician—or a psychiatrist. But right now, I was going to hit the sack.

My hand went out automatically and switched the light off.

"Damn!" I thought incredulously. I'd shorted the dynamo again. The radio stopped as if the whole orchestra had dropped dead; every light in the cabin winked swiftly out, but my hand on the switch crackled with a phosphorescent glow as the entire house current poured into my body. I tingled with weird shock; I heard my own teeth chattering.

And something snapped wide open in my brain. I heard, suddenly, an excited voice, shouting.

"Rhys! *Rhys!* That is the man!"

RAINBOW CITY

"*You are mad,*" said the man with the tired voice.

I was drifting. I was swaying, bodiless, over a huge abyss of caverned space; chasmed, immense, limitless. Vaguely, through a sleeping distance, I heard two voices. This one was old and very tired.

"You are mad. They will know. Narayan will know. " "Narayan is a fool," said the second voice.

"Narayan is the Dreamer," the tired voice said. "He is the Dreamer, and where the Dreamer walks he will know. But have it your way. I am very old and it does not matter. I give you this power, freely—to spare you. But Gamine—"

"Gamine—" the second voice stopped. After a long time "You are old, and a fool, Rhys," it said. "What is Gamine to me?"

Bodiless, blind, I drifted and swayed and swung in the sound of the voices. The humming, like a million high-tension wires, sang around me and I felt myself cradled in the pull of a great magnet that held me suspended surely on nothingness and drew me down into the field of some force beneath. Far below me the voices faded. I swung free—fell—plunged downward in sickening motion, head over heels, into the abyss....

My feet struck hard flooring. I wrenched back to consciousness with a jolt. Winds blew coldly in my face; the cabin walls had been flung back to the high-lying stars. I was standing at a barred window at the very pinnacle of a tall tower, in the lap of a weird blueness that arched flickeringly in the night. I caught a glimpse of a startled face, a lean tired old face beneath a peaked hood, in the moment before my knees gave way and I fell, striking my head against the bars of the window.

I was lying on a narrow, high bed in a room filled with doors and bars. I could see the edge of a carved mirror set in a frame, and the top of a chest of some kind. On a bench at the edge of my field of vision there were two figures sitting. One was the old grey man, hunched wearily beneath his robe, wearing robes like a Tibetan Lama's, somber black, and a peaked hood of grey. The other was a slimmer younger figure, swathed in silken silvery veiling, with a thin opacity where the face should have been, and a sort of opalescent shine of flesh through the silvery-sapphire silks. The figure was that of a boy or a slim immature girl; it sat erect, motionless, and for a long time I studied it, curious, between half-opened lids. But when I blinked, it rose and passed through one of the multitudinous doors;

at once a soft sibilance of draperies announced return. I sat up, getting my feet to the floor, or almost there; the bed was higher than a hospital bed. The blue-robe held a handled mug, like a baby's drinking-cup, at me. I took it in my hand hesitated—

"Neither drug nor poison," said the blue-robe mockingly, and the voice was as noncommittal as the veiled body; a sexless voice, soft alto, a woman's or a boy's. "Drink and be glad it is none of Karamy's brewing."

I tasted the liquid in the mug; it had an indeterminate greenish look and a faint pungent taste I could not identify, although it reminded me variously of anis and garlic. It seemed to remove the last traces of shock. I handed the cup back empty and looked sharply at the old man in the Lama costume.

"You're—Rhys?" I said. "Where in hell have I gotten to?" At least, that's what I meant to say. Imagine my surprise when I found myself asking—in a language I'd never heard, but understood perfectly—"To which of the domains of Zandru have I been consigned now?" At the same moment I became conscious of what I was wearing. It seemed to be an old-fashioned nightshirt, chopped off at the loins, deep crimson in color. "Red flannels yet!" I thought with a gulp of dismay. I checked my impulse to get out of bed. Who could act sane in a red nightshirt?

"You might have the decency to explain where I am," I said. "If you know." The tiredness seemed part of Rhys' voice. "Adric," he said wearily. "Try to remember." He shrugged his lean shoulders. "You are in your own Tower. And you have been under restraint again. I am sorry." His voice sounded futile. I felt prickling shivers run down my backbone. In spite of the weird surroundings, the phrase "under restraint" had struck home. I was a lunatic in an asylum.

The blue-robed one cut in in that smooth, sexless, faint-sarcastic voice. "While Karamy holds the amnesia-ray, Rhys, you will be explaining it to him a dozen times a cycle. He will never be of use to us again. This time Karamy won. Adric; try to remember. You are at home, in Narabedla."

I shook my head. Nightshirt or no nightshirt, I'd face this on my feet. I walked to Rhys; put my clenched hands on his shoulders. "Explain this! Who am I supposed to be? You called me Adric. I'm no more Adric than you are!"

"Adric, you are not amusing!" The blue-robe's voice was edged with anger. "Use what intelligence you have left! You have had enough sharig antidote to cure a *tharl*. Now. Who are you?"

The words were meaningless. I stared, trapped. I clung to hold on to identity. "Adric—" I said, bewildered. That was my name. Was it? Wasn't it? No. I was Mike Kenscott. Hang on to that. Two and two are four. The circumference equals the radius squared times pi. Four rulls is the chemming of twilp—*stop that!* Mike Kenscott. Summer 1954. Army serial number 13-48746. Karamy. I cradled my bursting head in my hands. "I'm crazy. Or you are. Or we're both sane and this monkey-business is all real."

"It is real," said Rhys, compassion in his tired face. "He has been very far on the Time Ellipse, Gamine. Adric, try to understand. This was Karamy's work. She sent you out on a time line, far, very far into the past. Into a time when the Earth was different—she hoped you would come back changed, or mad." His eyes brooded. "I think she succeeded. Gamine, I have long outstayed my leave. I must return to my own tower—or die. Will you explain?"

"I will." A hint of emotion flickered in the voice of Gamine. "Go, Master." Rhys left the room, through one of the doors. Gamine turned impatiently to me again. "We waste time this way. Fool, look at yourself!"

I strode to a mirror that lined one of the doors. Above the crimson nightshirt I saw a face—not my own. The sight rocked my mind. Out of the mirror a man's face looked anxiously; a face eagle-thin, darkly moustached, with sharp green eyes. The body belonging to the face that was not mine was lean and long and strongly muscled—and not quite human. I squeezed my eyes shut. This couldn't be—I opened my eyes. The man in the red nightshirt I was wearing was still reflected there.

I turned my back on the mirror, walking to one of the barred windows to look down on the familiar outline of the Sierra Madre, about a hundred miles away. I couldn't have been mistaken. I knew that ridge of mountains. But between me and the mountains lay a thickly forested expanse of land which looked like no scenery I had ever seen in my life. I was standing near the pinnacle of a high tower; I dimly saw the curve of another, just out of my line of vision. The whole landscape was bathed in a curiously pinkish light; through an overcast sky I could just make out, dimly, the shadowy disk of a watery red sun. Then—no, I wasn't dreaming, I really did see it—beyond it, a second sun; blue-white, shining brilliantly, pallid through the clouds, but brighter than any sunlight I had ever seen.

It was proof enough for me. I turned desperately to Gamine behind me. "Where have I gotten, to? Where—*when* am I? Two suns—those mountains—"

The change in Gamine's voice was swift; the veiled face lifted questioningly to mine. What I had thought a veil was not that; it seemed to be more like a shimmering screen wrapped around the features so that Gamine was faceless, an invisible person with substance but no apprehensible characteristics. Yes, it was like that; as if there was an invisible person wearing the curious silken draperies. But the invisible flesh was solid enough. Hands like cold steel gripped my shoulders. "You have been back? Back to the days before the second sun? Adric, tell me; did Earth truly have but one sun?"

"Wait—" I begged. "You mean I've travelled in time?"

The exultation faded from Gamine's voice imperceptibly. "Never mind. It is improbable in any case. No, Adric; not really travelling. You were only sent out on the Time Ellipse, till you contacted some one in that other Time. Perhaps you stayed in contact with his mind so long that you think you are he?" "I'm not Adric—" I raged. "Adric sent me here—"

I saw the blurring around Gamine's invisible features twitch in a headshake. "It's never been proven that two minds can be interchanged like that. Adric's body. Adric's brain. The brain convolutions, the memory centers, the habit patterns— you'd still be Adric. The idea that you are someone else is only an illusion of your conscious mind. It will wear off."

I shook my head, puzzled. "I still don't believe it. Where am I?"

Gamine moved impatiently. "Oh, very well. You are Adric of Narabedla; and if you are sane again, Lord of the Crimson Tower. I am Gamine." The swathed shoulders moved a little. "You don't remember? I am a spell-singer." I jerked my elbow toward the window. "Those are my own mountains out there," I said roughly. "I'm not Adric, whoever he is. My name's Mike Kenscott, and your hanky-panky doesn't impress me. Take off that veil and let me see your face."

"I wish you meant that—" a mournfulness breathed in the soft contralto. A sudden fury blazed up in me from nowhere. "And what right have you to pry for that old fool Rhys? Get back to your own place, then, spell-singer—" I broke off, appalled. What was I saying? Worse, what did

I mean by it? Gamine turned. The sexless voice was coldly amused. "Adric spoke then. Whoever sits in the seat of your soul, you are the same—and past redemption!" The robes whispered sibilantly on the floor as Gamine moved to the door. "Karamy is welcome to her slave!"

The door slammed.

Left alone, I flung myself down on the high bed, stubbornly concentrating on Mike Kenscott, shutting out the vague blurred mystery in my mind that was Adric impinging on consciousness. I was not Adric. I would not be. I dared not go to the window and look out at the terrifying two suns, even to see the reassurance of the familiar Sierra Madre skyline. A homesick terror was hurting in me.

But persistently the Adric memories came, a guilty feeling of a shirked duty, and a frightened face—a real face, not a blurred nothingness—beneath Gamine's blue veils. Memories of strange hunts and a big bird on the pommel of a high saddle. A bird hooded like a falcon, in crimson.

Consciousness of dress made me remember the—nightshirt—I still wore. Moving swiftly, without conscious thought, I went to a door and slid it open; pulled out some garments and dressed in them. Every garment in the closet was the same color; deep-hued crimson. I glanced in the mirror and a phrase Gamine had used broke the surface of my mind like a leaping fish. "Lord of the Crimson Tower." Well, I looked it. There had been knives and swords in the closet; I took out one to look at it, and before I realized what I was doing I had belted it across my hip. I stared, decided to let it remain. It looked all right with the rest of the costume. It felt right, too. Another door folded back noiselessly and a man stood looking at me.

He was young and would have been handsome in an effeminate way if his face had not been so arrogant. Lean, somehow catlike, it was easy to determine that he was akin to Adric, or me, even before the automatic habit of memory fitted name and identity to him. "Evarin," I said, warily.

He came forward, moving so softly that for an uneasy moment I wondered if he had pads like a cat's on his feet. He wore deep green from head to foot, similar to the crimson garments that clothed me. His face had a flickering, as if he could at a moment's notice raise a barrier of invisibility like Gamine's about himself. He didn't look as human as I.

"I have seen Gamine," he said. "She says you are awake, and as sane as you ever were. We of Narabedla are not so strong that we can afford to waste even a broken tool like you."

Wrath—Adric's wrath—boiled up in me; but Evarin moved lithely backward. "I am not Gamine," he warned, "And I will not be served like Gamine has been served. Take care." "Take care yourself," I muttered, knowing little else I could have said. Evarin drew back thin lips. "Why? You have been sent out on the Time Ellipse till you are only a shadow of yourself. But all this is beside the point. Karamy says you are to be freed, so the seals are off all the doors, and the Crimson Tower is no longer a prison to you. Come and go as you please. Karamy—" his lips formed a sneer, "If you call *that* freedom!"

I said slowly "You think I'm not crazy?"

Evarin snorted. "Except where Karamy is concerned, you never were. What is that to me? I have everything I need. The Dreamer gives me good hunting and slaves enough to do my bidding. For the rest, I am the Toymaker. I need little. But you—" his voice leaped with contempt, "you ride time at Karamy's bidding—and your Dreamer walks—waiting the coming of his power that he may destroy us all one day!"

I stared somberly at Evarin, standing still near the door. The words seemed to wake an almost personal shame in me. The boy watched and his face lost some of its bitterness. He said more quietly "The falcon flown cannot be recalled. I came only to tell you that you are free." He turned, shrugging his thin shoulders, and walked to the window. "As I say, if you call that freedom."

I followed him to the window. The clouds were clearing; the two suns shone with a blinding brilliance. By looking far to the left I could see a line of rainbow-tinted towers that rose into the sky, tall and capped with slender spires. I could distinguish five clearly; one, the nearest, seemed made of a jewelled blue; one, clear emerald green; golden, flame-colored, violet. There were more beyond, but the colors were blurred and dim. They made a semicircle about a wooded park; beyond them the familiar skyline of the mountains tugged old memories in my brain. The suns swung high in a sky that held no tint of blue, that was as clear and colorless as ice. Abruptly I turned my back on it all. Evarin murmured "Narabedla. Last of the Rainbow Cities. Adric—how long now?"

I did not answer. "Karamy wants me?" Evarin's laugh was only a soundless shaking of his thin shoulders. "Karamy can wait. Better for you if she waited forever. Come along with me, or Gamine will be back. You don't want to see Gamine, do you?" He sounded anxious; I shook my head. Emphatically, I did not want to see that insidious spook again. "No. Why? Should I?"

Evarin looked relieved. "Come along, then. If I know Gamine, you're pretty well muddled. Amnesiac. I'll explain. After all—" his voice mocked, "you are my brother!"

He thrust open the door and motioned me through. Instinctively I drew back, gesturing him to lead the way; he laughed soundlessly and went, and I followed, letting it slide shut behind me.

We went down stairs and more stairs. I walked at Evarin's side, one part of me wondering why I was not more panicky. I was a stranger in a world gone insane, yet I had that outrageous calmness with which men do fantastic things in a dream. I was simply taking one step after another; knowing what to do with that part of me that was Adric. Gamine had spoken of habit patterns, the convolutions of the brain. I had Adric's body. Only a superficial me, an outer ego, was still a strange, muddled Mike Kenscott. The subconscious Adric was guiding me. I let him ride. I felt it would be wise to be very much Adric around Evarin. We stepped into an elevator shaft which went down, curved around corners with a speed that threw me against the wall, then began, slowly, to rise. I had long since lost all sense of direction. Abruptly the door of the shaft opened and we began to walk along a long, brilliantly illuminated passage. From somewhere we heard singing; a voice somewhere in the range of a trained boy's voice or a woman's mature contralto. Gamine's voice. I could make no sense of the words; but Evarin halted to listen, swearing in a whisper. I thought the faraway voice sang my name and Evarin's, but I could not tell. "What is it, Evarin?"

He gave a short exclamation, the sense of which was lost on me.

"Come along," he said irritably, "It is only the spell-singer, singing old Rhys back to sleep. You waked him this time, did you not? I wonder Gamine permitted it. He is very near his last sleep—old Rhys. I think you will send him there soon." Without giving me a chance to answer—and for that matter, I had no answer ready—he pulled me aside between recessed walls and again the shaft in which we stood began to ride. Eventually we stepped into a room at the top of another tower, a room lavishly, even garishly furnished. Evarin flung himself carelessly on a divan embroidered in silken purple and gestured me to follow his example. "Well, now tell me. Where in Time has Karamy sent you now?"

"Karamy?" I asked tentatively. Evarin's raucous laugh rang out again. He said with seeming irrelevance, but with an odd air of confiding "My one demand of the Dreamer is—freedom from that witch's spells. Some day I shall fashion a Toy for her. I am not the Toymaker of Narabedla for nothing. I demand little enough of the Dreamers, Zandru knows! I do not like to pay their price, but Karamy does not care what she pays. So—" he made a spreading movement of his hands, "she has power over everyone, except me. Yes; assuredly I must make her a Toy. She sent you out on the Time Ellipse. I wonder who brought you back?" I shook my head. "I've been out of my body too long. I can't remember much."

"You remember me," Evarin said. "I wonder why she left you that? Karamy's amnesia-rays took the rest of your memory. She never trusted me that far before."

But I caught the crafty look in his face. I knew only this about Evarin; Karamy was right not to trust him. I said "I only remember your name. Nothing more."

Because Evarin—I knew—was never ten minutes the same. He would profess friendship and mean friendship; ten minutes later, still in friendship, he would flay the skin from my body and count it only an exquisite joke. I did not like those perverted and subtle eyes. He seemed to read my thought. "Good, we will be strangers. Brothers are too—" he let the word trail off, unfinished. "What have you forgotten?"

Could I trust him with my terrible puzzlement? How much could I, as Adric— and I must be Adric to him—get along without knowing? What was even more to the point, how many questions could I dare ask without betraying my own helplessness? I compromised. "What are the Dreamers?"

That had been the wrong question.

"Zandru. Adric, you have been far indeed! You must have been back before the Cataclysm! Well—our forefathers, after the Cataclysm, ruled this planet and built the Rainbow Cities. That was before the Compact that killed machines. Some people say the Dreamers were born from the dead machines."

He began to pace the floor restlessly. "They were men—once," he said, "They are born from men and women. Mendel knows what caused them. But one in every ten million men is such a freak—a Dreamer. Some say they came out of the Cataclysm; some say they are the souls of the dead Machines. They are human—and not human. They were telepaths. They could control everything—things, minds, people. They could throw illusions around things and men—they contested our rules."

He sat down; his voice became brooding, quiet. "One of us, here in Rainbow City, a dozen generations ago, found a way to bind the Dreamers," he said. "We could not kill them; they were deathless, normally. But we could bind them in sleep. As they slept, under a forced stasis, we could make them give up their powers—to us. So that we controlled the things they controlled. For a price." There was a glimpse of horror behind his eyes. "You know the price. It is high."

I kept silent. I wanted Evarin to go on.

He shivered a little, shook his head and the horror vanished. "So each of us has a Dreamer of his own who can grant him power to do as he wills. And after years and years, as the Dreamers grow old, they grow mortal. They can be killed. And fewer are born, now; fewer to each generation. As they grow older and weaker, it is safe to let them wake; but never too strongly, or too long." He laughed, bitterly. A fury came from nowhere into his face.

"And you loosed a Dreamer!" he cried. "A Dreamer with all his power hardly come upon him! He is harmless as yet—but he wakes, and he walks! And one day the power will come upon him—and he will destroy us all!" Evarin's thin features were drawn with despair; not arrogant, now, but full of suffering. "A Dreamer—" he sighed, "A Dreamer, and you had been made one with him already! Can you see now why we do not trust you—brother?"

Without answering I rose and went to the window. This window did not look on the neat little park, but on a vast tract of wild country. Far away, curious trails of smoke spiralled up into the sunlight and a wispy fog lay in the bottomlands. "Down there," said Evarin in a low voice, "Down there the Dreamer walks and waits! Down there—"

But I did not hear the rest, for my mind completed it. Down there—

Down there is my lost memory. Down there was my life.

Somewhere down there I had left my soul.

FLOWERS OF DANGER

I turned my back on the window. "Rhys is a Dreamer," I said with slow certainty. "What is Gamine?"

Evarin nodded slowly, ignoring the question. "Rhys is a Dreamer, yes. He is old—so old he is almost mortal now; so he wakes, and he too walks. But he was one of us once—the only Dreamer ever born within the Rainbow City. His loyalty is double; but he will never harm Narabedla, because he is of our blood." Evarin cleared his throat. "So Gamine takes what knowledge can be had from his old, old mind. And does not pay."

"Who is Gamine?" I asked again. Evarin still hesitated.

"Karamy hates Gamine," he said, after minutes. "So no man sees Gamine's face. I would not ask too many questions—unless you ask them of Karamy." A smile flickered on the mobile features, "Ask Karamy," he said gleefully, "She will tell!"

"She will?" I said stupidly, because I could think of nothing else to say. Evarin's grin was delicately malicious. "Oh, I am sure of that! Karamy is quick to strike. Gamine and I have little love lost, but we agree on one thing; that Karamy's procession of slaves is monstrous. And that you are a fool to help Karamy pay for her—desires. Karamy is far too fond of power in her own hands, to pay to put it into yours."

Karamy. Karamy who took my memory—

"She did." Evarin murmured, and I realized I had spoken aloud. The room seemed full of a weighty silence. Evarin's prowling footsteps made no noise as he came to my side. "I can give it back to you, though. I have made you a Toy." His effete voice rather disgusted me, and I moved away, but he followed. "Look here, and find your memory."

And he put something small and hard into my hand; something wrapped in silvery silks.

I raised my hand curiously, untwisting the wrappings. They were smooth and shining and colorless, with a bluish cast, like Gamine's veils; no fabric I had ever seen. Evarin backed slowly away from me. For an instant all I could see was a blurred invisibility—like Gamine's face behind the veils—then a sort of mirror became slowly visible, It did not seem to reflect anything; rather, it was a coldly shining surface, cloudy, glittering from within. I bent to examine the pattern of the shadows that moved on the surface. There was a curious pull from the mirror, a cold that crept sluggishly from my hand. A familiar, soothing cold. As if drawn by a magnet, my eyes bent closer—

Recognition crashed in my mind. Evarin—and his gilt deadly Toys.... I dashed the colorless thing to the floor, giving it a savage kick. The blurred invisibility wavered; I caught a glimpse of a tiny jewelled mechanism, before it sprang back to gray ice again. Evarin had backed halfway across the room; I leaped at him, collaring the dandy and wrenching him close. "I've a good mind to tie the thing across your throat!" I grated.

Evarin's lip twisted up. Suddenly his whole face melted in a blurring invisibility and I felt his whole substance evaporate from between my hands. He writhed like smoke, and I leaped backward just as he materialized, whole and deadly, too close. "I am always—guarded!" he jerked out at me, "I might have known—"

He stooped, reaching for the fallen toy. I kicked the little mirror out of his reach, bent to retrieve it. "I'll keep this," I said, and wadding the insulated silk around it, I thrust it into a pocket. Evarin's eyes glared at me helplessly. "You'll stay solid for awhile now," I jeered. "*Toymaker*! Damned freak—" I stormed out of the room, leaving him rubbing his bruised shoulder.

Now that Adric was back in control, I had no trouble discovering where I wanted to go. Some blind instinct led me through the maze of elevators and staircases; I stepped into servant's quarters, kitchens, a roomful of buzzing machinery I dismissed with a glance of familiarity; and finally found myself in the open, the semicircle of rainbow towers around me.

Overhead the suns, red and white, sent a curious, double-shadowed light downward through the neatly-trimmed trees. A little day moon, smaller than any moon I had known, peeped, a curious crescent, over the edge of a mountain. The grass under my feet was just grass, but the brightly-tinted flowers in mathematically regular beds were strange to me. Paths, bordered by narrow ditches to keep the pedestrian off the flowers, wandered in and out of this strange pleasaunce; I accepted all this without conscious thought, but some unconscious scrap of memory gave me a vague practical reason for the ditches. I carefully avoided them.

Faint shrill music tugged siren-like at my ears; wordless, like Gamine's crooning. Staring, I realized that the flowers themselves sang. The singing flowers of Karamy's garden—I remembered their lotus song. A song of welcome? Or of danger?

I was not alone in the garden. Men, kilted and belted in the same gaudy red and gold as the flowers, passed and repassed restlessly, unquiet as chained flames. For a moment the old vanity turned uppermost in my mind. For all her slaves, all her—lovers, Karamy paid tribute to the Lord of the Crimson Tower! Paid—would continue to pay!

The men passed me, silent. They were sworded, but their swords were blunt, like children's toys; they were a regiment of corpses, of zombies. Their salutes as I passed were jerky, mechanical.

A high note sang suddenly in the flowers; I felt, not heard, their empty parading cease. In a weird ballet they ranged themselves into blind lines that filed away nowhere; toy soldiers, all alike.

And between the backs of the toy-soldiers and the patterned, painted flowers, I saw a man running. Another me, from another world, thought briefly of the card-soldiers, flat on their faces in the Red Queen's garden. Wonderland. I heard myself say, with half-conscious amusement "They all look so alike until you turn them over!"

The man running between the ditched flower-beds was no dummy from a pack of cards. I saw him beckon, still running. He called to me; to Adric. "Adric! Karamy walks here—just listen to the flowers! I was afraid I'd have to get all the way into the tower to find you!" His voice was urgent, breathless; he slid to a stop not three feet from me. "Narayan knew they'd freed you! He's outside the gates. He sent me to help. Come on!"

The sight of the man touched another of those live-wires in my brain; the name of Narayan, another still. "Narayan—" I said in dull recognition. The word, on my lips, hit a chord of fear, of dread and danger—

But I had come straight from Evarin. I knew the man; I knew the response he expected, but the brief glimpse into Evarin's mirror had set up a chain of actions I could not control. I tried to put out my hand in friendly greeting; instead I felt, with horror, my fingers at my belt and tried, without success, to halt the sword that flew without volition from its sheath. The man backed away, his eyes full of terror.

"Adric—no—the Sign—" he held up one arm, deprecatingly, then howled with agony, clutching the severed fingers. I heard my own voice, savage, inhuman, the thin laughter of Evarin snarling through it. "Sign?? There's a sign for you!"

The man threw himself out of range; but his face, convulsed with pain, held a stunned bewilderment. "Adric—Narayan promised—you were sane—" he breathed.

I forced my sword back into the scabbard, staring without comprehension at the blood from the wound I had inflicted, and at the darting heads of the flowers. I could not kill this man who carried the name of Narayan on his tongue.

The flowers twitched—stirred—threw tendrils at the man's bleeding hand. A quick nausea tightened my throat; I motioned urgently to him.

"Run!" I begged, "Quick, or I can't—"

The flowers shrilled. The man threw back his head, his eyes wide with panic, and screamed.

"Karamy! Aiiieeeee—!" he staggered back wildly, teetering on the edge of the ditch. I cried another warning, incoherent—but too late. He trod on the flowers— stumbled across the little ditch. The writhing flower-heads shot up shoulder-high. They screamed a wild paean of flower-music, and he fell among them, sprawling, floundering helplessly. I heard him scream, hoarsely, horribly—I turned my eyes away. There was a wild thrashing, a flailing, a yell that died and echoed among the brilliant towers. There was a sort of purring murmur from the blossoms.

Then the flowers stilled and were quiet, waving innocently behind their ditches. Karamy, gold and fire, walked along the winding path through the trees. And in the space of a second I forgot the man who lay lifeless in the bed of the terrible flowers.

Karamy was all gold. From her glowing crown of hair to the tips of her little slippers, she was one sunny shimmer; there was amber on her brows and at her throat, and an amber rod twisted lightly between her fingers, its delicate movement outlining my face. Karamy's smile of welcome was a dream which made me know I could be well content if this were my world.

But old habit made me turn my face away; her eyes, cat-eyes of wide yellow, watched me slyly, but her face was turned to the sprawled man in the flowers. "So? I thought I heard—something." Without taking her eyes from my face, she spun the lucent rod. The flower-song rose again, a soft keening wail. Two of the silent guards moved noiselessly through the garden, and at an expressive movement of the rod, they lifted the corpse and bore it away. The music died. The woman's hands went out to pull me close.

"Adric, Adric! As soon as you are free, they pursue you! That is not what you want, is it?"

"Isn't it?" I asked shortly. I still could not look full at the cat-eyes, the caressing face. A memory scuttled, rabbit-fashion, across my mind, giving name and identity to the man I had betrayed to the flowers.

Karamy slid in front of me so I had to look at her, and the lovely lazy voice murmured the name I was beginning to know. "You are angry," the soft voice caressed me, "I knew it was not right to let Evarin near you! Adric, we need you, Narabedla needs you! We felt betrayed when you left us, when you shut yourself up alone with your stars! Have you forgotten, or are you still—my lover?"

It rang phony! Phony, was the way I put it to myself. Part of me felt like calling her a lying she-devil and having that much, at least, on record. But I was fast acquiring a double cunning. The animal cunning of Adric's old habit—and a desperate, trapped cunning of my own, born of a desperate fear of this unfamiliar world. There was nothing I could do except ride on the surface and let my hunches take me where they would. Karamy was very soft and sweet and something more than lovely in my arms and I held her crushingly close while I struggled with a memory. Who was Karamy? Who—and what—was I?

Karamy dropped her arms. The mantle of lazy seductiveness dropped with them. She spoke with eager annoyance. "You are still angry because I sent you on the Time Ellipse! You do not know it was for your own good—you haven't learned your lesson yet—"

That talk meant danger for me. I could think of only one way to silence it. She seemed to like it; but even with her lips acquiescent under mine, I was wary. Was I fooling her—or was she only playing my own game, and playing it a little better?

"Now we can make plans," she said a little later, "First, Gamine." She looked sharply at me, but I kept my face expressionless. "Gamine is always with the old Dreamer; she lets him wake; he will grow too strong. We must send Rhys away from Narabedla. Gamine may stay or follow him to exile. But Rhys must go."

"Rhys must go," I conceded. "He should be slain, but Gamine will never do it," said Karamy with a shrug that disposed of Rhys.

"Evarin—" she snapped her jewelled fingers. "His Dreamer sleeps sound! Evarin fears even his own power! My Dreamer grows strong—but he serves me!" The beautiful face looked ruthless and savage. "Your Dreamer walks—free in the forest! Only you can re-bind him. You, with my help—Adric of the Crimson Tower!"

Her eyes smoldered. "Yes, and my Dreamer shall serve you as well, till then!" She breathed. "I will pay to put power in your hands!" The very phrase Evarin had used! A shudder stung me briefly.

Her glowing face burned through my sting of fear. "I go to the Dreamer this night, Adric! Ride with me, and he shall lead you where the Dreamer walks—and lead you back to power! I have said enough—" the lambent eyes tilted at me, "Have I not?"

She had, and too much. For I knew now how the Dreamer must be paid. And the small part of me that was still Mike Kenscott cowered; the rest of me accepted the memory with a shrug. It was this Adric part that spoke. "I'll go. And afterward, I'll go into the forest where the Dreamer walks—and bring him back to you!"

But even as I swept Karamy into my arms and bent her head back roughly under my mouth, a warning prickle iced my spine. I said, insinuatingly "And then, Karamy——" but my eyes narrowed over her golden head.

Karamy had tricked me before this.

TRAPPED!

Afterward, when I had found my way back to the Crimson Tower, I searched for hours for something that might give a clue to Adric's mystifying past. I was puzzled about this Adric who came and went as he pleased in the chambers of my memory. But I found nothing; whoever had stolen Adric's memory, had made sure that nothing in his surroundings should clear up the puzzle in his mind. I knew only one thing. Adric was feared, disliked, distrusted by all the Narabedlans, and all except Gamine had something to gain by feigning friendship. I could not decide whether Karamy's attitude was love that pretended contempt to mold Adric, or me, to her will, or contempt that pretended love for the same reason. And although habit found affection for Evarin, I could not trust him long. Trust a cyclone sooner than that half-mad effeminate! The name, Narayan, stuck burr-like in my mind. Friend, or enemy? I sat at the barred window of Adric's high room, trying to force memory from the alien mind in which I was prisoner. And whether it was sheer effort of will, or the result of the fragmentary look in Evarin's mirror, or whether, as Gamine insisted, I was really Adric and Mike Kenscott was a mere superficial illusion of my conscious mind, memory did begin to pulse back.

In the early days....

In the early days, before the vagueness came on my mind, I, Adric of the Crimson Tower, had been a power in the Rainbow City. The memories of that time were not the kind Mike Kenscott would have cared to own, but I, as Adric, found them vastly pleasing. Unlike Gamine, who loved only knowledge, or Evarin, who toyed with pleasure and trickery, I had wanted power. I had it, unlimited, from a Dreamer who stirred only vaguely in sleep. Half the known portions of this world had known the Crimson Tower as lord. And Karamy—

Some memories were triumphant. Some were humorous in Adric's cynical mind. Some were terrible beyond guessing—for Adric had not counted cost, and even he shuddered from the price the Dreamer had exacted.

Then, to this wilful and wild man, something had happened. I had no idea what; Karamy had reached that far back and blurred, though not entirely erased, my memory. It had something to do with a blonde boy's face, lifted in incredulous terror—or joy; and a fleeing form, veiled, that retreated down the long corridor of my mind, averting its face as I followed. Whatever had happened, it had come when Adric was sick with blood and horror, when he was surfeited, even if momentarily, with conquest, and sickened at the price the Dreamer extorted. The power, forced through the mind of the Dreamer, called for energy; kinetic energy, available from one source and one only. Adric had fed the Dreamer with that power. For a while.

One day, as a whim, I had redeemed a young woman slave—then the vagueness came and choked me. I might think; I might burst my brain, but so far and no farther my memories would carry me. I could not force memory of that chain of events. But after that, Adric's reign had collapsed like the unstable arch it had been. His armies scattered, and he had shut himself up or been imprisoned in his Tower; his memories had been stolen and he had gone, or been sent, spinning along a time line forward, or perhaps back, until somewhere in the abyss of time he touched Mike Kenscott.

It had been then, perhaps, that Adric had escaped. He had reached, drawn Mike Kenscott back—and switched the two. It was a perfect escape from a life Adric had come to hate.

But I was Adric. There was an explanation for that, too. The physical body could not make the transit in time. I had Adric's body; the convolutions of his brain, the synaptic links of habit. His memory banks. Only the Ego, the superimposed pattern of the conscious identity, insisted I was Mike Kenscott. In Adric's body, the old patterns ruled, and to all intents and purposes, I was Adric. And back in my own time, I thought, Adric was living in my body—living Mike Kenscott's life, going through the motions, with only the same queer lapses I was making here. And after a while, even these would stop. I was wholly trapped. Here, living Adric's life, the part of me that was Adric would grow stronger and stronger till—he?— unseated the other identity wholly. And he, in my body? Andy, I thought with a wild swift fear, *what will he do to Andy?*

Nothing. He could not hurt Andy—not in my pattern—any more than I could hate Evarin. Or could he?

I had to get back! God, I *had* to get back!

When the white sun had set and the red sun glowed a darkening ember across the Sierra, a summons came, brought by one of Karamy's toy-soldier cohorts. I dressed—in crimson again, for there was no other clothing anywhere—and followed the voiceless sentry down through a labyrinth of elevators, finally emerging into a long corridor. I strode down it, hearing my own steps echo; a second rhythm joined them imperceptibly, and Gamine stole out of the darkness, swathed in the luminous veiling, creeping noiselessly as a ghost behind me. Later I became conscious of Evarin's padding cat-steps behind Gamine, trailing us, single-file. And other figures came from darkened recesses to stretch the silent parade; a slim girl in a winged cloak, flame color; a dwarfed man who walked beneath the amethyst huddle of purple cap and furs. Memory fitted names to them, but I did not speak to them, or they to me.

After a long time, the immense corridor began to tilt upward, climbing toward a glimmer of light at the end. Without realizing it I had swung into an arrogant, loping stride; now I brushed away the slave-soldier who headed the column and took the lead myself. Behind me the others fell into place as if I had bidden them; the flame-clothed girl in the winged cloak, the cat-footed Evarin, the dwarf bent in his jester's cap, Gamine in the blue shroud. Without warning, we came out into a vast court; an enclosed space, yet wide as the outdoors, a yard, a plaza, a place of imposing grandeur. A place of memory.

The red sun above us glowed like a lurid coal. There were tall pillars on three sides of the courtyard, and at the far end, a vaulted archway led into a treelined drive that stretched away for miles into the twilight. Between two pillars, Karamy waited; slim, shimmering golden from head to foot. A hungry impatience sparked in her cat's eyes. "You're late." "I'm ready," I said. What I was ready for, I was not sure. Karamy waved an impatient signal to the Narabedlans who were coming up. "Adric is with us again," she said in her curious lazy voice, "Your allegiance to Adric—children of the Rainbow!"

I stood at her side, mute, waiting; a guard of silent men behind us. "Lord Idris;" Karamy summoned. The hunchback came to bow jerkily before us. "Welcome home—Lord!"

The girl in flame-color darted to where we stood and her dipping curtsy was like the waver of a moth toward a flame. "Adric—" she murmured. The wings of her cloak lifted and fluttered across her shoulders as if they would fly of themselves. She was a shy thing, and her dark hair waved softly as if it too were winged. I touched her fingers lightly, but under the smolder of Karamy's gaze I let her go. She watched me, shyly, with averted face.

Evarin's face was slyly malicious, but his voice was pure silk. "It is—pleasure to follow you again, my brother," he almost purred, and I scowled at the mockery at his face and refused his offered hand. Only Gamine said nothing, coming forward on gliding feet to bow briefly and retire; but the silver-sweet, sexless voice of the spell-singer murmured in a singing, almost wordless, croon. "Save your spells, Gamine," said Karamy savagely, and Evarin jerked round at the shrouded form, but Gamine heeded neither of them, and the sweet contralto chanting went on.

From somewhere the silent men brought horses. Horses—here, in this nightmare world? I had never been on a horse in my life. I found myself vaulting, with a nice coordination of movement, into the saddle. The courtyard, for all the bustle of department, seemed to hold the silence of a grave. Karamy kept me close to her. When we were all mounted, she threw the amber rod upward, and the last rays of the red sun caught its rays and sent a pure shaft of light down the darkened alley-way lined with trees. At the sight of that gleam, a curiously familiar emotion stole through me. I threw up one arm over my head, mimicking Karamy's gesture. "Ride!" I shouted.

And the flying steeds kept pace with mine.

The driveway under the arch of trees led for miles under the thick boughs. Through the easy drumming of hooves, I could still hear the sweet distant sound of Gamine's singing, which floated on the wind, keeping pace with the rise and fall of the rolling road, in a quick cadence. The wind whipped Karamy's golden hair like a halo about her head. I glanced over my shoulder to where the rainbow towers stood, now black, silhouetted against the greater darkness of the mountains. Over-head in the pink sky, the crescent of the tiny moon was brightening, and lower in the sky I saw another, wider disc, nearly at full. Cold air was stinging my cheeks and nipping my bones with frost, and I felt the sparks struck from hooves beating on the frozen ground.

Cold! Yet in Karamy's garden flowers had glowed in a tropical glory—

And for a moment, it was entirely Mike Kenscott—sick, bewildered and panicky—who glanced about him with horror, feeling the swirling cold and a colder chill from the golden sorceress at my side. It was Mike Kenscott's will that jerked at the reins of the big gelding to end this farce now— "What is it?" Karamy cried, over the noise of the hooves.

And I heard my own voice, raised above the galloping rhythm, cry back "Nothing!" and call out a command to the horse.

Good God! I was Mike Kenscott—but prisoner in a body that would not obey me—a mind that persisted in thoughts and habits I could not share, a—soul?— that would carry me to destruction! I was Mike Kenscott—trapped on a nightmare ride through hell!

WHERE THE DREAMER WALKS

I had been scared before. Now I was panicked, wild with a nerve-destroying fright. I'm not a coward. I set up a radar transmitter in Okinawa within ninety feet of a nest of Japs. That was something real. I could face it. But under two suns and a pair of little moons, with weird people I knew were not human—all right; I was a coward. I steadied myself in the saddle, trying with every scrap of my will to calm myself. If this was a nightmare, well, I'd had some beauties—

But it wasn't. I knew that. The frost hurting my face, the sound of shod steel on stones, the vivid colors around me, told me I was wide awake. Dreams are not technicolored. And through all this I was riding hell-for-leather, my knees gripped on the saddle, guiding the horse with the grip of my thighs—and I'd never been on a horse's back in my life. Rode—and rode—

We had ridden about seven miles, and stopped twice to breathe the horses, but we were still beneath the great archway of trees. The sky's pink sunset light had faded; the land was flooded with a blue, fluorescent starlight, a light I'd never seen before. I strained my eyes upward through the black foliage. I suppose I had some confused idea of guessing when I was by the stars. But the view to the North was hidden by mountains, and I don't know one constellation from another, with that single exception. A glance at Karamy, in this fright, un-nerved me; I touched the reins, dropped back till I rode between Gamine and the girl in flame-color. "Adric," the spell-singer saluted coolly, and the girl in the winged cloak threw back her hood; I saw dark eyes watching me from a pure, sweet young face. Before the luminous innocence of those eyes I wanted to cry out in protest. I was not Adric, warlock of Narabedla. I was just a poor guy named Mike, I was just—me. I rode beside Gamine for minutes, trying to think what I would say.

Gamine's musical voice was not raised, yet it carried perfectly to my ears. "You seem wholly yourself again."

I didn't answer. What was there to say? Still, there seemed to be sympathy in the sharply-edged tones. "You will remember—perhaps too much—at the Dreamer's Keep."

"Gamine," I asked, "Who is Narayan?"

I saw the blue robes quiver a little; across from Gamine, I saw a curious flickering look pass across the face of the girl in the orange winged cloak.

But Gamine's answer was perfectly even and disinterested. "The name is not familiar to me. Have you heard it, Cynara?"

The girl did not answer, only moved her dark head a little.

"I should know," I mused. But the name Cynara had touched another of those live wires within my mind. Narayan. Cynara. Cynara and Narayan! If I could only remember! Suddenly I turned. "Gamine—who are you?" Gamine sat quiet, eerily motionless on the tall horse. The robed figure seemed to blend into the starlit shadows around us. I had the sudden feeling of having re-lived this moment before, then the veiled shoulders twitched impatiently.

"Is this an inquisition?"

Rebuked, and stung by the arrogant voice, I touched my heel to my horse's flank and rode forward to rejoin Karamy. Gamine! The hell with Gamine!

For several minutes the road had been climbing, and now we topped the summit of a little rise and abruptly the trees came to an end. By tacit consent we all drew our horses to a walk. We stood atop the lip of a broad bowl of land, perhaps thirty miles across, filled to the brim with thick dark forest. Far out in this valley lay a cleared space, and in the center of that space lay a great tower; but not a slender and fairylike spire like the Towers of Rainbow City. This was a massive donjon thrusting heavy shoulders upward into the moon-washed sky.

The Keep of the Dreamers.

Something in me murmured "This is the forest where the Dreamer walks!"—or had the murmured voice come from Gamine, motionless behind me? Karamy rode eagerly, her face drawn tautly together, her slim tanned hands clenched on the reins. All this while I was Mike Kenscott—but a Mike who watched himself without knowing what he would do next, like those puzzling nightmares where a man is both actor and audience to some mummery being played. I watched myself say and do things as if I were two men at once. In effect, I suppose I was.... Karamy turned in her saddle, facing me.

"Adric," she murmured, "Lead me where the Dreamer walks!" I knew, with a sudden surety, that because of some bond between the freed Dreamer and myself, I could do this. But again, something outside myself told me what to say. "That bond is broken, Karamy. Did you not break it yourself? How can I guide you then?" And for my reward I saw unsureness leap in her cat's eyes. That shot had told. Karamy had been guessing, then! The answer had shaken her. But this woman was a past mistress at subtlety. She murmured "It can be forged again. That I swear."

Ah, but I knew how far to trust even Karamy's oaths!

We had dipped down into the bowl of forest and we were riding through thick woods, along a road that struggled windingly, with many curves and sharp corners. Adric knew this country; his knowledge made Mike Kenscott shiver. He had hunted here, and for no fourlegged game. As if Karamy read my thoughts I hear her low laughter. "So. My wrist aches for the feel of a falcon. We'll hunt here again—soon, you and I!" I was partly bewildered by her words, but they gave me a shivering excitement, an insidious thrill.

Behind me, I heard Gamine's chanting take on a new note. The words were still indistinguishable, but the very tune screamed warning. A pulse began to twitch jerkily in my neck.

Without any warning, the road twisted. Karamy and I spurred our horses and rounded the curve in one swift, racing burst of speed——and were fairly in the trap before we knew it.

It was the agonized whinny of my horse, and the jolt of my body righting itself automatically from the plunging animal beneath me, that made me realize we had ridden straight on a chevaux-de-frise. I yelled, cursing, shouting to Karamy to get back, get back, but her own momentum carried her on; I saw her light body fly out of the saddle and disappear. The others, rounding the curve in a wild dash, were fairly on the barrier already, and the place was a bedlam, a scramble, with riderless horses milling in a melee of curses and the screaming of women and the threshing of feet. I was out of my saddle in an instant, thrusting Gamine's mount back from the stabbing points fixed invisibly against the dark barrier in the road, shouting to Evarin and Idris. Evarin leaped to my side, catching at Karamy's wild horse, while I tore madly at the barrier where the woman had been thrown. Idris bore down on me, mounted. "Go round!" he shouted. I plunged through the underbrush at the side of the road, with hasty feet twice snaked by long creepers. Past the barrier, the road lay open and deserted, and Karamy lay in a shimmer of crumpled silk, motionless. "Gamine, Evarin—" I bellowed, "No one's here! Quick, Karamy is hurt—"

The head and shoulders of Idris' horse thrust through the thick brushwood. "Is she dead?" the dwarf muttered. I bent, thrusting my hand to her breasts. "Her heart's beating. Only stunned. Get down," I ordered. Idris scrambled, monkey-fashion, from the saddle. I lifted the woman in my arms, but she did not move or open her eyes. Idris touched my arm.

"Put her on the saddle," he suggested, and together we laid her across the pommel. Suddenly, the dwarf cried out.

"What?" I asked sharply.

"I hear—"

I never knew what Idris heard. His head vanished, as if snatched away by a giant's hand; a rough grip collared me, choking fingers clawed at my throat, a thousand rockets went off in my head and I lay sprawling in the brushwood, eating dust, with an elephant sitting on my chest and threatening hands gouging my throat. My last coherent thought before the breath went out of me, was—

"I'm waking up!"

NARAYAN

But I wasn't. When I came to—it could only have been a few seconds that I was unconscious—it was to hear Evarin snarling curses and Idris barking incoherently with rage. I heard Karamy screaming my name, and started to answer, but the steely fingers were still at my throat and with that weight on top of me, I hadn't a chance. The fall, or something, had knocked Adric clean out of me. I was fuzzy-brained, but sane. I was an innocent bystander again.

I could see Evarin and Idris in the road, casting wary glances at the brushwood all around them. I could just make out the face of the man who was holding me pinned to the earth with his body. He had the general build of a hippopotamus and a face to match. I squirmed, but the threatening face came closer and I subsided. The man could have broken me in two like a match.

Around me in the thicket were dozens of crouching forms, fantastic snipers with weapons at their shoulders. Weapons that could have been crossbows or disintegrators, or both. "Enter Buck Rogers," I thought wearily. I was beginning to feel faint again, and old welter-weight on my stomach didn't help any. Abruptly he moved, delicate fingers knotting a gag in my gasping mouth; then the intolerable weight on my chest was suddenly gone and I sucked in air with relief. The fat man eased himself cautiously up, and I felt a steel point caress my lowest rib. The threat didn't need words. I could see the Narabedlans gathered, a tight little knot in the road. The snipers around me were still holding their weapons, but the fat man commanded in a low voice "Don't fire! They're sure to have guards riding behind them—" the voice died to a rasping mutter, and I lay motionless, trying to dredge up some of Adric's memories that might help; but the only thing I got was a fleeting memory of my own football days and a flying tackle by a Penn State halfback that had knocked me ten feet. Adric was gone; clean gone.

The Narabedlans were talking in low tones, Gamine the rallying-point round which they clustered. Evarin had his sword out, but even he did not step toward the mantling thicket. Cynara was holding Evarin's arm, protesting wildly. "No, no, no, no! They'll kill Adric—"

Suddenly, between two breaths, the road was alive with mounted men. Who they were, I never knew; I was quickly dragged to my feet and jerked away. Behind me I heard shouting, and steel, and saw thin flashes of colored flame. Spots of black danced before my eyes as I stumbled along between two captors. I felt my sword dragged from my scabbard. Oh well, I thought wryly, now that Adric's run out on the party I don't know how to use it anyway. Under the impetus of a knife I found myself clambering awkwardly into a saddle, felt the horse running beneath me. There wasn't a chance of getting away, and the frying pan couldn't be much worse than the fire, anyway.

Behind us the noises of battle died away. The horse I rode raced, sure-footed, into the darkness. I hung on with both hands to keep from falling; only Adric's habitual reflexes kept me from tumbling ignominiously to the ground. I don't think I had any more coherent thoughts until the jolting rhythm broke and we came out of the forest into full moonlight and a glare of open fires.

I raised my head and looked around me. We were in a grove, tree-ringed like a Druid temple, lit by watch-fires and the waver of torches. Tents sprouted in the clearing, giving it an untidy, gypsy appearance; at the back was a white frame house with a flat roof and wide doors, but no windows.

Men and women were coming out of the tents everywhere. The talk was a Pentecost of tongues, but I heard one name, repeated over and over again.

"Narayan! Narayan!" the shouts clamored.

A slim young man, blond, dressed in rough brown, came from one of the larger tents and walked deliberately toward me. The crowd drew back, widening to let him approach; before he came within twenty yards he made a signal to one of the men to untie my gag and let me down. I stood, clinging to the saddle, exhausted; the young man came forward until he could almost have touched me, and studied my face dispassionately. At last he raised his head, turning to the fat man, my captor.

"This isn't Adric," he said. "This man is a stranger."

I should have been relieved; I don't know why I wasn't. Instead, my first reaction was bewilderment and angry annoyance. How could he tell that? I was as furiously embarrassed as if I'd been accused of wearing stolen clothing. My beefy captor was as angry as I was. "What do you mean, this isn't Adric?" he demanded belligerently, "We took him right out of their accursed cavalcade! If it isn't Adric, who is it?"

"I wish I knew," Narayan muttered under his breath. His eyes, still fixed on my face, were level, disconcerting. He was tall and straightly built, with pale blond hair cut square around his shoulders like a squire from a Provencal ballad, and grey eyes that looked grave, but friendly. I liked his looks, but he had a trace of the uncanny stillness I'd noticed in old Rhys, in Gamine. For a moment I decided to tell my whole fantastic story to this man with the grave eyes. He would surely believe it. But to my surprise, he spoke and called me Adric; definitely, as if he had forgotten his doubts. "Adric," he said, "Do you still remember me? Or did Karamy take that too?"

I sighed. I didn't dare tell the truth, and I felt too chilled and exhausted and disoriented to lie convincingly. Yet lie I must, and do it well.

The fat man scowled and fronted Narayan. "Karamy—Zandru's eyelashes!" he growled. "Look you, did Brennan come back this afternoon? He knows his way around Rainbow City. Ask Adric what happened to Brennan!"

The clamoring broke out around us again, but Narayan never took his eyes from my face as he answered gently "There is always danger, Raif. Blame no man unjustly. Brennan knew he faced all the dangers of Rainbow City. And even Adric is not to blame if a she-witch has him under her spells." "Traitor!" Raif snarled at me and spat.

I loosed the saddle-horn and stepped dizzily forward. "You might try asking me," I said with a weary anger.

"Are you Adric of the Crimson Tower?" fat Raif snapped.

"I don't know—" I said tiredly. "I don't know, I don't know!"

Narayan's eyes met mine in puzzlement. Abruptly he put out one hand and took my wrist in a firm grip. "We can't talk here, whoever you are," he said. "Come along."

He led me through the thinning crowd into the frame house at the grove's edge; Raif and one other man trailed after us, the rest clustering hive-fashion around the door. Inside, in a great timbered room, a fire burned and glowing globes chased away darkness. I went gratefully toward the fire; I was stiff with riding and I felt chilled and stupid and empty with the cold. From a wood settle near the fire, a woman rose. She was slight and dark and around her shoulders the luminescent shimmer of her winged cloak flowed like another flame. Cynara.

"Adric—" she said half-aloud, holding out her hands. I took them, partly because she seemed to expect it, partly because the girl seemed the only thing real in a world gone haywire. She flung her arms suddenly around my neck and held herself to me with a shy deliberation. "Adric, Adric, Adric—" she begged, "I slipped away in the dark—I suppose Gamine knows—but they'll never find me here, no, never—"

Narayan's hand pulled the girl sternly away from me; she shrank before the annoyance in his eyes. "Please—Narayan, no—"

The blond man looked at her without speaking for long moments. At last he said gravely "Sister, you must go back to Narabedla. I would not make you go if there was another way; but you must, for a time." He beckoned to one of the men. "Kerrel—" he commanded, "Take Cynara back to Rainbow City, but don't get caught. Cynara; tell them you were lost in the woods, or that you were caught and escaped."

The childish mouth trembled, and she turned to me appealingly, but I gave a little shrug. What was I supposed to do? Narayan gave Cynara a gentle push. "Go with Kerrel, little sister," he ordered in a quiet voice; Kerrel took her arm and they hurried out of the room, the winged cloak she wore fluttering on her shoulders. Narayan motioned to Raif to follow them through the door. "I'll talk with him alone."

Raif's thick lips set stubbornly. He looked as if he'd be nasty in a fight. "If he's Adric, and if he's under Karamy's devilments, then—"

"I have faced Adric, and Karamy too," said Narayan with a friendly grin at the man. "Get out, Raif; you're not my bodyguard, or even my nurse!"

The fat man accepted dismissal reluctantly, and Narayan came to my side. There was real friendliness in his grin. "Well," he said, "Now we will talk. You cannot kill me, any more than I could kill you, so we may as well be truthful with each other. Why did you leave us, Adric? What has Karamy done to you this time?"

The room reeled around me. I put out a hand to steady myself—when the dizziness cleared, Narayan's arm was around my shoulders and he was holding me up with a strength surprising in his slight frame. He let me settle down on the seat Cynara had left. "You have been roughly handled," he said in apology, "Just sit still a minute. My men—" he made a deprecating little gesture, "have had orders. And if I know Karamy's ways, you've been heavily drugged for a long time." His eyes studied me intently. "Better come and have a drink. And—when did you eat last? You look half starved. That's the way of the sharig—"

I rubbed my forehead. "I can't remember," I told him honestly.

"I thought so. Come along." Narayan went into the next room, assuming that I would follow and that I knew my way around. After the insanely furnished rooms in Rainbow City, I was a little surprised when the next room proved to be a strictly functional and ordinary kitchen, equipped with the usual items. Out of a relatively un-extraordinary icebox he assembled something that looked rather like the food I was accustomed to from the 20th century, and poured some kind of liquid into an oddly shaped glass. He motioned me into a chair and set the things on the table. "Here, eat this. I know the drugs they give you; you'll have more sense when you've eaten. We've plenty of time to talk, all night if we choose." He saw me glance sidewise at the glass, laughed sketchily, and from the same bottle poured himself a drink and sat down opposite me, sipping it slowly. "Go ahead. I won't poison you till I find out what Karamy's up to."

I laughed apologetically and started eating, with a mental shrug. It had been at least forty-eight hours since I had last tasted food, and I did justice to the plateful before me. Narayan sipped his drink—which, when I tasted mine, appeared to be excellent cognac—and watched me; and when I finally pushed the empty plate aside, he put back his glass and said "Now. Who are you, and what happened?"

I felt better and stronger; more like myself than I'd felt since Rhys had catapulted me into this world. But now that I was on the carpet, I felt I must talk fast and convincingly before those searching grey eyes.

"Karamy had me shut in the Tower," I told him, "I was freed today, and we were on our way to the Dreamers Keep. Then your men came along. I didn't know if I was being rescued or captured. I still don't." I stared with purposeful blankness at Narayan; he stared back and I could feel him debating what to do and say. Obviously, an Adric sane and glib and possibly untruthful was a different thing than an Adric too bewildered and shaken to tell anything but the truth. Finally Narayan said "I'm not sure what I ought to do or say, Adric. The bond between us isn't as strong as it was. You know that."

I nodded, perturbed. Adric's thoughts seemed to be surging back, insidiously, as if Narayan held the key to unlock them. What crazy drama was going to be unfolded in my mind now?

Narayan said, low; "Karamy did it, I think."

"Yes." My own voice was as quiet as his own. "Karamy sent me on the Time Ellipse. She knew I'd come back changed—or mad—or not at all. I think—I think she wanted me to betray you again."

"Adric!" Narayan reached out quickly and grabbed my arm, hard, above the elbow, till I cried out with the pain of that steely grip and twisted away, rubbing numbed flesh. "Adric—" Narayan repeated, unsteadily, "Why do you say—betray me again? Betray me? Adric—it was your hand that freed me! Zandru! Adric—" he begged, "*How much* have you forgotten?"

BATTLE IN MY BRAIN

The fire in the other room had burned down to an ember. Without a glance my way, Narayan mended the fire; sat down, his legs stretched toward the little blaze, his shin in his hands; waiting. I could not stand still. I walked, restless, around the room, speaking in little jerks and half-sentences.

"You are the Dreamer," I said, "I—I remember a little. I remember being bound to you. I remember when I—freed you. Not knowing what it might mean, not knowing you could have slain me on the ground of sacrifice."

"No!" Narayan was as motionless as Gamine's veils, but his voice was harsh, strident. "No, Adric, never that! We cannot—kill each other, you and I. I could order you killed, I suppose, but I—I would never do that unless there was no other way. Adric—is there any other way for me, for you?"

A bitterness spoke in my voice; neither side trusted Adric, both wanted his allegiance. I tried to trim my words carefully between the two personalities that were battling for mastery in me.

"It was Karamy," I said, "who took Adric from you, and sent him, half-mad, back to the Crimson Tower. Karamy's magic stripped him of power, and sent him, gone mad, back to stargazing in Narabedla. But it was not Karamy's—" the voice that was not quite mine shook, suddenly, with my own weariness and the blank terror I'd been keeping at bay, "It wasn't Karamy who sent me here, I'm not Adric. You were perfectly right. I'm no more Adric than—than you are. I'm in Adric's body, yes. He moves me like a puppet! I have his memories, his—some of his thoughts—but he—" my voice cracked suddenly on a note of panic; I knew I sounded like a hysterical kid, but I couldn't stop my own crackup once it had broken loose. "I'm not Adric, I'm not! I don't belong here at all! I don't—"

Narayan jumped up from the bench and I heard his hurrying steps, then his steel hands were hard on my shoulders, swinging me around to face him. "All right," he said, "Steady. It's all right."

I drew a long breath and let it out again. "Thanks," I said briefly, shamed. "I'll be all right now."

Narayan shrugged wearily. "It's all right. I guessed you weren't Adric, of course, from the beginning. But I didn't think Adric, when it came to the test, would really do that to me. I had his promise. I suppose, for him, it was an easy way out. A perfect way of escape." He sank down on the bench again, dropping his head in his hands. After a little, he looked up, and his voice sounded tired. "This is difficult," he said. "My men think you are Adric. I'd never be able to convince them you aren't. Would you mind—pretending? You'll have to; otherwise—" he paused, and I saw disquiet in his face. He was not a man who would enjoy threatening, but I could understand his situation. They didn't know me from Adam; I was just an out-sider who messed things up by resembling Adric. Well, I was stuck. I hadn't liked the Narabedlans enough to give a hang what Narayan meant to do to them. Narayan, by comparison, looked pretty decent. And there was no other way to save my skin. Adric wasn't too popular, it seemed and in Adric's body I hadn't a chance. I laughed. "I'll try," I told him. "But what's this all about?"

Narayan looked up again. "That's right. You wouldn't know. You have some of Adric's memory, I suppose, but not all. You remember who I am?"

"Not entirely—" I told him. I remembered some things. Narayan had been born, some thirty years ago, into a respectable country family who were appalled to discover they had given birth to a mutant Dreamer, and were only too glad to deliver him to the Narabedlans for the enforced stasis. I told Narayan.

"You remember the old Dreamer who served your House?"

I nodded. He had become old, mortal, weak—and had been eliminated. I bowed my head, although I had no personal guilt.

Afterwards, Narayan and I had been bound. "I slept in the Dreamer's Keep—" Narayan sounded reflective, almost guilty, "I was wakened, and—given sacrifice. I learned to use my power and to give it up to Adric." A brooding horror was in the grey eyes; I realized that Narayan dwelt in his own personal private hell with the memory of what he had done under the spell of Narabedla. "Adric was—strong."

Yes, I thought; Adric had called on Narayan's new power without counting cost. What wonder the memory maddened Narayan? The young Dreamer seemed to win his silent fight for self-control. "Well, you—Adric, I mean—freed me. I found my sister again; Cynara. I was like a child; I had to learn to live, to be alive again. I had been trained to use my power only through the Sacrifice. I had to learn to use it without. It wasn't easy."

"Why?" I asked thoughtlessly. Narayan's eyes froze me. "To use that power," he said in a tense, controlled voice, "Took human life."

*

Outside the door I could hear the noises of the camp; the light of their watchfires crept in through the cracks. It was too dark to see Narayan's face now, but I heard him moving restlessly about the room. "I have harnessed the power somewhat," he said, "I can use it, myself, a little. Not much. Adric helped me; so did my sister. She had been taken for Sacrifice, but you—Adric—redeemed her. Then—we were able to throw an illusion around Cynara. She is not of Narabedla; but we made it seem as if she had always been there, in Rainbow City. We could do that because Evarin is weak, and because Karamy did not care. It was Rhys who made the Illusion."

"Rhys!" The old Dreamer, the only one born in Narabedla—

"Yes; Gamine is careless with Rhys and lets him wake too long. Rhys and I have been in contact for a long time."

I was hearing scraps of conversation from a vast abyss of time and space, when I had been drawn in electric coma through Karamy's Time Ellipse. They will know, Narayan will know. That had been old Rhys. And Adric; What have I to do with Narayan? Adric had been—still was—playing a fancy double game with Narayan; I started to open my lips to tell the young Dreamer about it, but he was still talking. "Rhys will not act, not directly, against Rainbow City. But he did that much for us, and Gamine and Cynara are friends. We forgot—we all forgot—that Adric's allegiance belonged to Narabedla first. Until he vanished." I heard the brooding heaviness in Narayan's voice. These men had been friends. Narayan went on, "I sent Brennan today, to find out. He didn't come back." I lowered my head and miserably told him what had happened to Brennan. Narayan's face in a flicker of firelight looked drawn and haggard. "He was a—brave man," Narayan said at last. "But I don't blame you. After the interchange, I think, there was a time when you went on living Adric's life. Thinking his thoughts. But now, I think, he will grow weaker in you. I hope. You—who are you, in your own world?"

I shrugged. The words would have meant nothing to Narayan. "My name's Mike Kenscott."

"Mi-ek," Narayan repeated, turning the strange word on his tongue. "The men will call you Adric. I'd better, too. Later—" he shrugged. I didn't say anything; I was still convinced that I hadn't seen the last of Adric. But I didn't want to tell Narayan this. I liked the man.

Without warning, Narayan switched on lights. "It's near dawn, and you must be worn out. We've taught them to stay clear of the forests at night, so we're safe enough here. They can't do much till they've been to the Dreamers Keep, in any case." With a sudden boyish friendliness he put out his hand and I took it. "I'm glad you're not Adric. He might be hard to handle now—if he's changed so much." As if the lights had been a signal, fat Raif came without knocking into the room. Narayan crossed his hostile stare at me. "He's all right, Raif," the Dreamer said. The fat face broke into a sudden, elephantine smile. "I'd better apologize, Adric. I had orders."

"Find him a place to sleep," Narayan suggested, and I followed Raif up a flight of low stairs into an inner room. There was a bed there, clean, but tumbled as if it had had another occupant not long ago. Raif said "Kerrel's gone with Cynara. You can sleep here."

I kicked off my boots and crawled between the blankets, suddenly too weary even to answer. I had been two days without sleep, and most of that time I had been under exhausting physical and mental strain. I saw Raif cautiously finger his weapons and sensed that whatever Narayan said, he was reserving judgment. He didn't take chances, this outsize lieutenant of Narayan's. Sleepily I said "You can put that up, my friend. I'm not going to move till I've had a good, long—"

I didn't even finish the sentence to myself. Instead I went to sleep.

I had slept for hours. I came abruptly out of confused dreams to hear a shrill voice and to feel small hands pulling me upright. Cynara! "Wake up, Adric—" she wailed, "Karamy and Evarin are riding today—hunting you!"

I sat up, dizzy-brained, far from alert. "Cynara! How—"

"Oh, never mind that—" her voice was impatient, "What can we do?" I didn't know. I was still stupid with sleep, but I put a reassuring arm around her shoulders. "Don't be afraid," I told her, then, releasing her, bent and began to pull on my boots. I heard the swift pound of steps on the stairs, and Narayan shoved open the door, dragging a brown tunic over his head as he came. He stopped short at the door, staring at his sister. "Cynara, what are you doing here?"

She repeated her news, and he sighed. He looked as if he hadn't slept at all. "Well, never mind," he told her, "The game was almost over, anyhow. Sooner or later they would have broken through the Illusion; Rhys is too old now for that. You were lucky to get away. We'll have to storm the

Keep tonight—unless they have too-good hunting." He fumbled with the laces of his shirt. A dead weariness was in his grey eyes; they looked flat, almost glazed. He met my questioning stare and smiled ruefully. "The Dreamers stir," he told me, "I am not yet free of—their need. So I must be careful." Cynara shuddered and threw her arms around her brother's neck, clutching him with a fiercely sheltering clasp. "Narayan, no—oh, no—don't—"

But he was already deep in thought again. He freed her arms without impatience. "We'll meet that when the time comes, little sister. So Karamy and Evarin ride hunting. Who else. Idris?" At her nod, his brows contracted. "All of them—but Gamine," he mused, and turned to me. "Could you conceivably get through to Rhys? I don't dare—not with that—that stirring."

I understood, Narayan was still attuned to the terrible need of the sleeping Dreamers in the Keep. But I reminded him that only Gamine could control old Rhys. He looked at me with a strange curious question in his eyes, but made no comment. My own mind was working strong. I was unsure how I had gotten here in the house of the freed Dreamer. Just what had happened last night? I had thought Narayan would never trust me again; but now, when I needed it most, I seemed to be in his complete confidence. Damn Karamy anyhow, meddling with my memory! And she had the audacity to fly Evarin's devil-birds after me—Adric, lord of the Crimson Tower! She should have a lesson she would not forget—and so should the presumptuous Gamine—and so should this walking zombie who was staring at me stupidly, as if I were his equal! I said with a slow savagery "I think I can manage Gamine!"

Narayan was watching me anxiously. Gods of the Rainbow, what preposterous things had I said and done last night? I said "We'll take them at the Dreamer's Keep," and saw his face clear.

But what you do not know, Narayan, I added to myself with a secret satisfaction, *is that you will join them there!*

It never occurred to them to question, to wonder if Adric today were the Adric of last night. We went downstairs and snatched a quick breakfast; Cynara tore off her winged flame-color cloak and stuffed it wrathfully into the fireplace. Her coarse grey dress beneath it made her shy prettiness more striking than ever; Cynara was not Karamy, but she was a pretty thing; and Narayan could hardly fail to trust me when Cynara perched on the arm of my chair and ran her dainty fingers over the bruises on my face. "Your roughs nearly killed him!" she pouted at her brother.

"Oh, I'm not hurt," I smiled at her, making my voice gentle for her ear alone. But I scowled darkly into my plate; pushed the food away and strode out into the camp. Narayan shouted quickly, jumping up, sending his chair crashing to the floor, and he ran after me so that we went down the steps together. "Wait," he commanded in my ear, softly, "Don't forget, to them you're still a traitor!" He took my arm, and we walked through every row of tents together, Narayan's expression almost belligerent. I saw the faces of the men as they came from their improvised shelter, saw suspicion gradually give way to tolerance and then casual acceptance. Finally Narayan called to Raif. "Stick to him, will you, Raif? He's all right, but the men don't know it yet."

I glanced at Narayan. "Raif," I said tentatively, "Can you find me twelve men who know the way to Rainbow City and aren't afraid to come close to it?"

"I can," Raif said, and went to do it. I had to hide a smile. Before long I would win back the place my foolishness had lost. The idiot whose body I had shared briefly had almost put it beyond recovery, but in a way he had helped, too. His weakness had won Narayan's confidence. Well, one thing I knew, that futile idiot should not share the coming triumph. Nor should Narayan.

Narayan—fumbling in my pocket, I touched something smooth and hard. Evarin's mirror. Narayan, looking over my shoulder as I dragged it out, asked curiously "What's that?"

I pulled it out with a secret smile. "One of Evarin's toys. Look at it, if you like."

Narayan took it in his hand for a moment, without, however, untwisting the silk. "Go ahead," I urged, "Unwrap it." I might have sounded too eager. Abruptly Narayan handed it back. "Here. I don't know anything about Evarin."

I had to conceal my disappointment. With a feigned indifference I thrust it back into the pocket. It did not matter. One way or another, Narayan would lose. For Evarin and Karamy rode a-hunting today—and I knew what their game would be!

FALCONS OF EVARIN

I pulled my cloak closer about me, prickling with excitement, as I knelt between Raif and Kerrel in the tree-platform. Just beneath me, Narayan clung to a lower branch. My ears picked up the ring of distant hooves on frozen ground, and I smiled; I knew every nuance of this hunt, and Evarin might find his deadly birds not so obedient to his call today. Not a scrap of me remembered another world where a dazed and bewildered man had flown at a living bird with his pocketknife.

Coldly I found myself considering possibilities. A snare there must be; but who: Narayan himself? No; he was my only protection until I got clear of this riffraff. Besides, if he ever unsheathed his power, unguarded like this, he could drain me as a spider sucks a trapped fly. No; it would have to be Raif. I had a grudge against the fat man, anyway. I pulled at his sleeve. "Wait here for me," I said cunningly, and made as if to leave the platform. Raif walked smiling into the trap. "Here, Adric! Narayan gave orders you weren't to run into any danger!"

Good, good! I didn't even have to order the man to his death; he volunteered. "Well," I protested, "We want a scout out, to carry word when they come." *As if we wouldn't know!*

"I'll go," Raif said laconically, and leaned past me, touching Narayan's shoulder. He explained in a whisper—we were all whispering, although there was no reason for it—and Narayan nodded. "Good idea. Don't show yourself."

I held back laughter. *As if that would matter!*

The man swung down into the road. I heard his footsteps ring on the rock; heard them diminish, die in distance. Then—

A clamoring, bestial cry ripped the air; a cry that seemed to ring and echo up out of hell, a cry no human throat could compass—but I knew who had screamed. That settled the fat man. Narayan jerked around, his blonde face whiter. "*Raif!*" The word was a prayer.

We half-scrambled, half-leaped into the road. Side by side, we ran down the road together.

The screaming of a bird warned me. I looked up—dodged quickly—over my head a huge scarlet falcon, wide-winged, wheeled and darted in at me. Narayan's yell cut the air and I ducked, flinging a fold of cloak over my head. I ripped a knife from my belt; slashed upward, ducking my head, keeping one arm before my eyes. The bird wavered away, hung in the air, watching me with live green eyes that shifted with my every movement. The falcon's trappings were green, bright against the scarlet wings.

I knew who had flown this bird.

The falcon wheeled, banking like a plane, and rushed in again. No egg had hatched these birds! I knew who had shaped these slapping pinions! Over one corner of my cloak I saw Narayan pull his pistol-like electro-rod, and screamed warning. "Drop it—quick!" The birds could turn gunfire as easily as could Evarin himself, and if the falcon drew one drop of my blood, then I was lost forever, slave to whoever had flown the bird. I thrust upward with the knife, dodging between the bird's wings. Men leaped toward us, knives out and ready. The bird screamed wildly, flew upward a little ways, and hung watching us with those curiously intelligent eyes. Another falcon and another winged across the road, and a thin, uncanny screeching echoed in the icy air. I heard the jingle of little bells. Three birds, golden-trapped and green-trapped and harnessed in royal purple, swung above us; three pairs of unwinking jewel-eyes hung motionless in a row. Beyond them the darkening red sun made a line of blackening trees and silhouetted three figures, ahorse, motionless against the background of red sky. Evarin—Idris—and Karamy, intent on the falcon-play, three traitors baiting the one who had escaped their hands.

The falcons poised—swept inward in massed attack. They darted between my knife and Narayan's. Behind me a bestial scream rang out and I knew one of the falcons, at least, had drawn blood—that one of the men behind us was not—ours! Turning and stumbling, the stricken man ran blindly through the clearing, down the road—halfway to those silhouetted figures he reeled, tripping across the body of a man who lay beneath his feet. Narayan gave a gasping, retching sound, and I whirled in time to see him jerk out his electro-rod, spasmodically, and fire shot after wild shot at the stumbling figure that had been our man. "Fire—" he panted to me, "Don't let him—he wouldn't want to get to—them—"

I struck the weapon down. "Idiot!" I said savagely, "Some hunting they must have!" Narayan began protesting, and I wrenched the rod from his hand. The man was far beyond firing range now. At Narayan's convulsed face I nearly swore aloud. This weak fool would ruin everything! I said hastily "Don't waste your fire! We can take care of them later—" I waved a quick hand at the three on the ridge. "There is no help for those caught by Evarin's birds."

Narayan breathed hard, bracing himself in the road. I beckoned the others close. "Don't fire on the birds," I cautioned, tensely; "It only energizes them; they drain the energy from your fire! Use knives; cut their wings—*look out!*" The falcons, like chain-lightning, traced thin orbits down in a slapping confusion of wings and darting beaks. I backed away from the purple-harnessed birds, flicking up my cloak, beating at the flapping wings. Our men, standing in a closed circle back to back, fought them off with knives and with the ends of their cloaks thrown up, swatting them off; and three times I heard the inhuman scream, three times I heard the lurching footsteps as a man—not human any more—broke from us and ran blindly to the distant ridge. I heard Narayan shouting, whirled swiftly to face him—he ran to me, beating back the green-trapped bird that darted in and out on swift agile wings. The screeing of the falcons, the flapping of cloaks, the panting of men hard-pressed, gave the whole scene a nightmare unrealness in which the only real thing was Narayan, fighting at my side. His gasp of inhuman effort made me whirl, by instinct, flinging up my cloak to protect my back, my knife thrust out to cover his throat. He raked a long gash across the down-turned head of the falcon, was rewarded with an unbirdlike scream of agony and the spasmodic open-and-shut of the razor talons. They raked out—clawing. They furrowed a slash in the Dreamer's arm. The razor beak darted in, ready to cut. I threw myself forward, unprotected, off balance, ready to strike.

At the last minute talons and beak turned aside—drew back—darted swiftly, straight at me. And my knife was turned aside, guarding Narayan!

But Narayan jerked aside. His knife fell in the road, and his arm shot out— grabbed the bird behind the head, twisting convulsively so the stabbing needle of a beak could not reach him. The darting head lunged, pecking at the cloak that wrapped his forearm; thrown forward, I stumbled against Narayan, carried by my own momentum, and we fell in a tangle of cloaks and knives and thrashing legs and wings, asprawl in the road. The deadly talons raked my face and his, but Narayan hung on grimly, holding the deadly beak away. I thrust with the knife again and again; thin yellow blood spurted in great gushes, splattering us both with burning venom; I snatched the wounded bird from the Dreamer's weakening hands twisted till I heard the lithe neck snap in my fingers. The bird slumped, whatever had given it life—gone!

And high on the ridge the dwarfed figure of Idris threw up his hands—fell— collapsed across the pommel of his saddle!

Narayan's breath went out limply in a long sigh as we untangled our twisted bodies. Our eyes met as we mopped away the blood. We grinned spontaneously. I liked this man! Almost I wished I need not send him back to tranced dream—what a waste!

He said, quietly "There is a life between us now."

I twisted my face into a smile matching his. "That's only one," I said. "The rest—" I turned, watching for a moment as the falcons tore at the ring of men. "Come on," Narayan shouted, and we flung ourselves into the breach. I flung down my knife, snatched a sword from someone and swung it in great arcs which seemed somehow right and natural to me. The men scattered before the sword like scared chickens, and I went mad with hate, sweeping the sword in vicious semicircles against the lashing birds ... the sword cut empty air, and I realized startlingly that both birds lay cut to ribbons at my feet, their blood staining the dead leaves. Narayan's eyes swam, through a red haze, into my field of vision. They were watching me, trouble and fright in their greyness. I forced myself to sanity; dropped the sword atop the dead birds. I wiped my forehead.

"That's that," I said banally.

We took toll of our losses, silently. Narayan, gasping with pain, rubbed a spot of the yellow blood from his face. "That stuff burns!" he grimaced. I laughed tightly; he didn't have to tell me. We'd both have badly festered burns to deal with tomorrow. But now, there was work—

"Look!" One of the men stared and pointed upward, his face tense with fright. Another great bird of prey hung on poised pinions above us, sapphire eyes intent; but as we watched, it wheeled and swiftly winged toward the Rainbow City. Not, however, before I had caught the azure shimmer of the bells and harness. A thin, sweet tinkling came from the flying bells, like a mocking echo of the spell-singer's voice.

Gamine!

THE RETURN OF ADRIC

Back in the windowless house, we snatched a hurried meal, cared for our slashed cuts, and tried to plan further. The others had not been idle while we fought the falcons. All day Narayan's vaunted army had been accumulating, I could hardly say assembling, in that great bowl of land between Narabedla and the Dreamer's Keep. There were perhaps four thousand men, armed with clumsy powder weapons, with worn swords that looked as if they had been long buried, with pitchforks, scythes, even with rude clubs viciously knobbed. I had been put to it to conceal my contempt for this ragtag and bobtail of an army. And Narayan proposed to storm Rainbow City—with this! I was flabbergasted at the confidence these men had in their young leader. So much the better, I thought, take him from them and they'll scatter to their rat-holes and crofts again! I felt my lips twisting in a bitter smile. They trusted Adric, too. When I had shown myself to them, their shouts had made the very trees echo. Well—again the ironic smile came unbidden, that was just as well, too. When Narayan was re-prisoned, I could use the power of their lost leader to tear down what he himself had built. The thought was exquisitely funny.

"What are you laughing about," Narayan asked. We were lounging on the steps of the house, watching the men thronging around the camp. His slumbrous grey eyes held deep sparks of fire, and without waiting for my answer he went on "Think of it! The curse of the Dreamer's magic lifted—what would it mean to this land, Adric? It means life—hope—for millions of people!"

In a way, Narayan was right. I could remember when I had shared that dream; when it had seemed somehow more worthy than a dream of personal power. Cynara came down the steps, bent and slipped her soft arms around my shoulder, and I drew her down. A volcano of hate so great I must turn my face away burned up in me. This man was my equal—no, I admitted grudgingly, my superior—and I hated him for it. I hated him because I knew that in his dream of power no one must suffer. I hated him because, once, I had been weak enough to share his feelings.

I said abruptly "Your plans are good, Narayan. There's just one thing wrong with them; they won't work. Storming Rainbow City won't get you anywhere. You could kill Karamy's slaves by the thousands, or the millions, or the billions. But you couldn't kill Karamy, and you'd only leave her free to enslave others. You've got to strike at them when they're in the

Dreamer's Keep. When the Dreamers wake is the only moment when they are vulnerable."

"But how can we get to the Dreamer's Keep, Adric? They go guarded a hundred times over, there."

"What's your army for?" I asked him roughly, "To knock down haycocks? Send your men to chase off the guards. I told you I could handle Rhys, if it came to that. He'll get us through to the Dreamer's Keep, if need be."

"What about Gamine?" Cynara asked practically. Gamine was the least of my worries, but I did not tell Cynara that. I listened to their comments and suggestions a little contemptuously. Didn't they know that when the Dreamers woke, the Narabedlans were vulnerable—to the Dreamers alone? If I were there with Narayan, there was no question about who would win.

Cynara scowled at the rip of talons across my face. "You're hurt and you never told me!" she accused. "Come this minute and let me take care of it!" I almost laughed. Me—Adric of the Crimson Tower—being ordered around by a little country girl! I snorted, but spoke pleasantly. "I'll live, I expect. Come and sit here with us." I pulled her down at my side, but she leaned her head on her brother's knee, an unquietness in her face. She was a pretty thing, although the cause of all my troubles. When I redeemed her from Karamy's slaves, for a whim, I had not known she was Narayan's sister—Zandru's hells, but I had made a ghastly slip! I had told Narayan there was no help for those touched by the birds, when I myself had redeemed his own sister! Had he noticed? Would he attribute it to Karamy's meddling with my mind? I smothered an exclamation, and Cynara and Narayan looked up anxiously. "You *are* hurt, Adric!"

I shook my head. I fancied Narayan looking at me with suspicion, but I controlled myself. I reached out to draw Cynara to me, but she had drawn back, rising lithely to her feet, like a dove poised for flight; only her hands, small darting hands like candle-flames, remained in mine to pull me lightly to my feet. I tried to hold her, but she protested "There is so much to be done—" and I raised the slim hands to my lips before I let her go. The gesture pleased her, I could see; so much that I watched with contempt as she tripped away. Silly, simple girl! It would please her!

In the end it was only Narayan and Cynara who rode with me to Rainbow City. Kerrel had taken the army, in sections, to set an ambush for Karamy's guards; we rode in the opposite direction, by a twisting side road. Cynara rode beside me, her dark eyes glowing. There was dainty witchery in Cynara, and a pretty trust that made me smile and promise recklessly "We will win." It pleased me to think that I could comfort Cynara for her brother's downfall. Once conditioned to Rainbow City, she would forget her silly fancies and be a fair and lovely comrade. If she continued to please me, it would be amusing to see this unformed country girl wield the power that had belonged to Karamy the Golden!

It took us an hour of hard riding to reach the lip of the great cup of land, where we paused, looking down the dark, almost-straight avenue of trees that led to the walls of Rainbow City. I whistled tunelessly between my teeth. "Whatever we do, it will be wrong. We'd be taking quite a chance to ride up to the main gate; at the same time, they'll be expecting us to sneak in the back way. They'd never expect us to come by the front avenue."

"The deer walks safest at the hunter's door," Narayan quoted laughing. "But won't they be expecting us to use that kind of logic?"

Cynara giggled, subsided at my frown. "At that rate," I said, "We could go on all night."

Narayan reached overhead, snatching down a crackling sheaf of frost-berries; selected one narrow pod. He held it between finger and thumb. "Chance. Two seeds, we go around. Three, we ride straight up the main gate. Agreed?" I nodded, and he crushed the dry husk. One, two—three seeds rolled into my outstretched palm. "Fate," Narayan said with a shrug. "Ready, then?"

I jounced the seeds in my palm. "One for Evarin, and one for Idris, and one for Karamy," I said contemptuously, and flung the little black balls into the road. "We'll scatter them like that!"

We were lucky; the drive was deserted. If there were guards out for us at all, they had been posted somewhere on the secret paths. Straight toward the towers we rode, under the westering red sun, and just before dusk we checked our horses and tethered them within a mile of the Rainbow City, going forward cautiously on foot.

I objected to this arrangement. "I'll get in alone," I told them. "If anything happens to me, we mustn't lose you as well!"

"I'll stay," said Narayan briefly. "If anything goes wrong, I'll be here to help." Silently I damned the man's loyalty, but there was nothing I could say without spoiling the illusion I had worked so hard to create. I took his hand for a minute. "Thank you." His voice was equally abrupt. "Good luck, Adric." Cynara glanced at me briefly and away again. I walked away from them without looking back.

It was easy enough to find my way into the labyrinthine towers. I was not Lord of the Crimson Tower without knowing its secrets. I climbed the stairs swiftly, ransacked the place. To no avail. When she took my memories, Karamy had also been careful to take everything which could conceivably give me any power over any of the Dreamers, even old Rhys. I went up more stairs till I stood at the very pinnacle of the tower, in Adric's star-room into which I had been catapulted—was it less than three days ago? I stood at the high window, vaguely thinking of an older Adric, an Adric who had watched the stars here, and not alone. I traced back through the years, diving down deep into the seas of sudden memory, and brought up the knowledge of—

"Mike Kenscott!" said a voice behind me, and I whirled to look into the face of a man I had never seen before.

He had the primitive look of a man out of some forgotten past. I had seen such men as I swam in the light of the Time Ellipse. He was tall and clean-shaven; he looked athletic; his eyes were a ridiculous color, dark brown. He had hair. He looked angry, if he could be said to have an expression.

But he spoke, clearly and with a deliberate calm. "Well, Mike Kenscott," he said, in a language I had never heard, but found myself understanding perfectly, "You have taken my place very nicely. I suppose I should thank you. You've given me freedom, and Narayan's trust—the rest I can do for myself!" He laughed. "In fact, you're so much *me* that I'm not much of myself. But I *can* force you back into your own body—"

The man must be mad! At any rate, he'd insulted the Lord Adric, in his own Tower, and by Zandru's eyelashes, he'd pay for it! I flung myself at him with a yell of rage. My fingers dug into his throat—

And I cried out in the stifling clutch of lean fingers grabbing at me, biting at my neck, my shoulders—an agonizing wrench shuddered over my body—

I faced—

Adric!

WHEN THE DREAMERS WAKE

Of course I understood, even while I fought, dizzy and reeling, to loose the deathgrip I had put on my own body. I was—back, I was Mike Kenscott again— Adric loosed his hands of his own will, and stepped away, breathing hard. "Thank you," he said in the raw voice that had been mine for so long, "I myself could hardly have done better." With a swift movement he snatched something from a little recess in the wall—pointed—and fired point-blank. A lance of grey mist stabbed out at me—

To my amazement, only a pleasant heat warmed me. I had enough split-second reasoning reflex left to fall in a slumped huddle to the ground. I knew that was what he expected. Adric fumbled in his pockets, took out the little mirror I had taken from Evarin, still wrapped in its protective silk. I watched, breathless, between narrowed eyelids. If he would only open it—but instead he gave a shudder of disgust and flung it straight at me. With a braced, agonizing effort I made myself lie perfectly still, without flinching to avoid the blow. The mirror struck my forehead. I felt blood break to the surface and trickle wetly down my face. I heard Adric moving; heard receding steps and the risp of a closing door. He was gone.

I moved. To this day I am not sure how I escaped death from Adric's weapon; but I think it was because I was in my own body. After I had touched Adric the first time, I was immune to Earth electricity. In this world, I think, I was immune to their force. I wiped the blood from my temple. Good Lord, there was Narayan—waiting with Cynara—I forgot that I had plotted against Narayan, remembering only that I had liked the man. I couldn't let Adric get to them—

I grabbed the mirror, crammed it into a pocket. Against the nightmare haste that drove me I ran to the closet, quickly, from the racks of weapons, chose a short ugly knife. I didn't need swordsman's training to use that. Thank God, I knew my way around, I could remember everything I'd done when I was Adric—but wait! I could also "remember" what he had done when he was me! That meant Adric could "remember" everything I had done and planned with Narayan! This crazy business of Identity! Even now, could I be sure which of us was who?

I dashed out of the room, ran down the endless stairs three at a time. At the entrance to Gamine's blue tower, a dangerous whirring of wings beat around me; I staggered, almost fell backward. One of the murderous falcons—the one in blue— darted, hanging poised in the stair-well above me. I backed against the wall, hoping the bird would not attack. Gamine had not flown falcon with the others.

The strong wings flapped in the closed space; I saw the dart of the vicious little beak. Blindly I struck upward with the knife, shielding my eyes with the other hand, and was rewarded with a splatter of thin burning blood and a scream of unbirdlike agony. I ducked beneath the thrashing wings, and ran on up the stairs; behind me the dying falcon flapped, threshed and rolled down the stairs, a tangle of wings, landing far below with a flailing thump.

I was not quite sure what I meant to do. As I climbed, I thought swiftly. Gamine was no friend to Adric, I knew that. Adric had known much of Gamine and Rhys, and I drew on that knowledge, but even Adric had not known much of the spell-singer cloaked in that blurred halo of invisibility. Had he ever seen Gamine?

What was Adric doing now? I had served him well; won him Narayan's trust, then turned him loose again in his own body, to destroy, betray them! I hated Adric as I hope I may never hate again.

And yet, I could not hate him wholly. To know all is to forgive much, and I had lived for three days and nights in Adric's body and brain; knowing his strengths and his weaknesses, his dreams and torments, I could not condemn him utterly. A man may be forgiven much that he does for a woman's bewitchments, and few men could be blamed for allowing Karamy to enslave them. Adric had done good, once, too; he had freed the Dreamer, he had loved—but he had trapped me here, and for that, my hate would make him pay—thoroughly!

A shadow flitted across my sight; the robed Gamine barred my way, an air of cold amusement around the poise of the hood and the blurred invisible head. The spell-singer laughed, mocking. "How like you this body, Adric? You are beaten now, for sure! The stranger works with Narayan—in your body, Adric!"

"I'm not Adric," I shouted. "Adric's in his own body again! He's going after Narayan—"

"You expect me to believe that?" Contempt stung me in Gamine's clear, sexless voice.

"Let me by to Rhys," I begged. "He'll know I'm telling the truth—damn it, let me by!" Infuriated by the mocking laughter, I thrust my arm to move

Gamine forcibly from my path. Whatever Gamine was—man, woman, imp or boy—it was not human. Steel wires writhed between my hands. I struggled impotently in that bone-breaking grip; then with a swift impulse thrust my hand quickly at the blurred invisibility where Gamine's face should have been.

Gamine screamed—a thin cry of horror. Suddenly I knew where I had been those two weeks I lay in the hospital—when Adric lay, in my body, gone mad, in the hospital in my place. An instinct I had grown to trust warned me to pull away sharply from Gamine's relaxed grip. I shouldered by and ran like hell. Halfway up the stairs I heard the spell-singer's feet running behind me, and I quickened my stride and sprinted for the heavy door that barred my way. I could feel Rhys' presence behind the door. I threw my weight against the door, twisting the handle frantically.

The door was locked.

Behind me, I heard the padding tread of Gamine. Hopelessly, I put my back to the door, pulling my knife out again, and defied the creature.

Behind me the door suddenly opened and I was flung backward, sprawling, into the room within. "Well, Mike," the old tired voice of Rhys said, "Gamine is a fool, but you are no better. Yes, I knew you were coming, I knew Adric is going, I know where Narayan is and I know what they plan to do. There is only one person who can stop all this, Mike Kenscott. You."

Gaping stupidly, I picked myself up from the floor. The old Dreamer, his wrinkled face serene under the peaked hood, watched me placidly. "What—how—" I stammered.

"Gamine is a prescient. And I am not a complete fool." Rhys smiled wearily. The dreamy look of the very old or the very young was on his face. "I cannot help you; but I will make Gamine help."

The spell-singer came into the room, and I could almost see resentment through that strange halo of nothingness. "Gamine," Rhys said, "it is time. You, and Narayan, must go with him to the Dreamer's Keep."

"No—" Gamine whispered in protest, "Narayan—cannot go! His—his—talisman was destroyed! Only outside the tower—he cannot go in!"

"There is still—mine. Give it to him." At Gamine's cry of dismay, Rhys' voice was suddenly a whip-lash. "Give it to him, Gamine! I still have power to—compel that! What does it matter what happens to me? I am old;

it is Narayan's turn; your turn." "I'll—keep it for Narayan—" Gamine faltered.

"No!" Rhys spoke sharply. "While you keep it—and I am bound to you—there is still the bondage. Give it to him!"

Gamine sobbed harshly. From the silken veils she drew forth a small jewelled thing; wrapped in insulating silk like Evarin's mirror. She untwisted the silk. It was a tiny sword; not a dagger, but a perfectly modelled sword, a Toy. Evarin's too; but different. I recalled that Evarin had called himself Toy-Maker. Gamine clung to it, the robed shoulders bent.

"Mike must take it," Rhys' voice was gentler. "If you keep it, I am still bound to you. If Adric had it, it would bind Narayan again. If Mike keeps it—near Narayan— Narayan is free. Free to go where he will, even in the Dreamer's Keep. Give it to him, Gamine." Rhys sat down, wearily, as if the effort of speech had tired him past bearing. I stood and listened with a rebellious patience; I was eager to be gone. But my eyes were on the little jewelled Toy in Gamine's hands. It winked blue. It shimmered. It pulsed with a curious heartbeat, hypnotic. Rhys watched, too, his tired face intent and almost eager. "Gamine; if Adric had seen you, had remembered—"

"I want him to remember!" Gamine's low wail keened weirdly in the silent room. Rhys sighed.

"I am Narabedlan," he said at last, "I could not destroy my own people. Gamine is not bound—nor you, Mike Kenscott. I suppose I am a traitor; but when I was born Narabedla was a fair city—without so many crimes on its head. Go and warn Narayan, Mike."

Gamine hovered near me, intent, jealous, the shrouded eyes fixed on Rhys. The old man spoke on in a fading voice. "My poor city—now, Gamine. Now. Give it to him and let me rest. Stand away from me, Mike; well away; I do not want the bondage again from you."

I did not understand and stood stupidly still. Gamine gave me an angry push. "Over there, you fool!" I reeled, recovered my balance, stood about six feet from the couch where Rhys half-sat, half-lay. The old man laid one wrinkled hand on the toy sword Gamine held. He took his hand away.

"Now," he said quietly.

Gamine thrust the sword into my hand, and I felt a sudden stinging shock, like electric current, jolt my whole body. I saw Gamine's robed body shiver with the same jolt. The Toy in my hand was suddenly heavy;

heavy as if it were made of lead, and the tiny winking in the hilt was darkened. The peaked hood of Rhys drooped until it covered the face.

Gamine caught my arm roughly and the steel of those narrow fingers bit to the bone as they hauled me almost bodily from the room. I heard the echo of a sob in the spell-singer's whispering croon.

Rhys—Farewell!

The next thing I knew we were racing side by side down flight after flight of stairs. Together we fled through the subterranean passages of Rainbow City. Outside, in the pillared court, a man ran toward us. His brown tunic was ripped and torn; his blond hair was rumpled. A smudge of blood reddened his forehead. I gasped "Narayan!"

The man whirled—saw us—pulled his weapon from his belt. There was no time for explanations. I threw myself at his knees in a flying tackle no football coach would approve, but it did the trick. Narayan went down under me, kicking. Gamine was not one to stand aside in a fight; the robed figure rocketed forward, flung itself on the prone Narayan, holding him motionless with that steely strength. I wrenched the electrorod from Narayan's relaxed fingers. "Listen—" I urged, "I'm not one of Karamy's men—Gamine, let him up!"

"He's got Cynara—" the Dreamer muttered dizzily, "Cynara—who in Zandru's hells are you?" He picked himself up, gazing at me with a stunned, blank look. "My name's Kenscott," I said briefly. Suddenly, feeling it was the best way to establish my good-faith, I pulled out the Toy Gamine had put in my hand. "I've seen Rhys. He sent—this."

Narayan stared at the thing in my hand, a double grief in his young face. "Rhys—" he muttered, "I felt he was—gone!" With bent head, he reached out to take the small thing from me.

In his hand it came alive. The small jewelled Toy seemed suddenly brilliant, flaring, dazzling with a wild burst of faceted light, blue, golden, crimson, flame-color. Gamine's low sweet voice breathed "In the Dreamer's hands!"

"In my hands," Narayan murmured in a choked, almost a tranced ecstasy. I broke in on their raptures rudely. "Here, Narayan! Is it Adric who's got Cynara?"

He gulped; swallowed hard; thrust the Toy into a pocket and came back to himself, but that light was still in his eyes. He spoke with a hard restraint. "Yes. Adric surprised me—knocked me out. When I came to, they were gone." He blinked once or twice; rubbed his eyes; then, resolutely fumbled for the little Toy and extended it to me. "Here. Keep this till we get to the Dreamer's Keep."

I took it without comment. Gamine slipped away; came back, leading horses. "I couldn't find a single guard," the cold voice murmured, "I wonder where they are?" "Adric knows," said Narayan, tight-lipped.

We mounted.

The wind was rising. Above us the moons swung slowly in an indigo sky. Sparks flew from our hooves against the frosty stones. We were racing against time, and a nightmare panic had me while I gripped the saddle of my racing horse. It took all my concentration to stick on the animal's back, but I was acquiring balance and a feel for riding. The ill wind was blowing some good, I thought inanely. Narayan's blond hair was frosty pale in the moonlight, and the eerie Gamine was a nightmare ghost, a phantom from nowhere. Far away we heard the spatter of gunfire, the screams of dying men, the ring of swords and spears. Thinly Gamine chanted in the night. Narayan's face looked haunted. "There are the guards—attacking—" he jerked out over the hoof-noises.

The scream of falcons rang swiftly above Gamine's chant. The too-familiar beat of wings slapped around my head, and I flung up my arm to knock away one serpentine neck. My terrified horse plunged and I rocked in the saddle nearly falling. Another bird swooped down on Narayan—another—then there were swarms of them, gold and purple and green, crimson, blue, flame-color. The air was thick with their wings. Gamine screamed; I saw Narayan beat the air with his cloak. The veiled spell-singer, crouched in the saddle, was lashing at them with the whip from her saddle. The lash kept the falcons at bay, but the razor talons caught at the blue shroudings. Narayan, whip in one hand, sword in the other, beat round him in great arcs, and I heard one bird's death-cry sending ringing echoes to the sky. I flung round me with my knife—

"The mirror—" screamed Gamine, "Evarin's mirror! Quick, they're coming by millions!"

They were coming in scores—hundreds, whirling and screeing. These were not the soul-falcons, belled and elaborately endowed with the intelligence and cunning of their launcher. These were—machines. Alive, yes, but not a life we knew. Only the nightmare freak of a science gone mad could produce—or control—these hateful things that were filling the clean air, groping for us with needle beaks and talons and wild wings. Only Evarin—

I fumbled blindly for the mirror, clumsily stripping the silks. A needle-talon raked at my wrist, and by sheerest instinct I struck upward, turning the face of the mirror toward the bird.

The bird reeled in mid-air—flapped—fell. A tingling shock rattled through my arm. I dropped the mirror—leaped to catch it. The thing was a perfect conductor. It—drained energy. I knew now why Evarin had been so anxious to have me—or Adric—look into its depths. It could have touched the energy waves of my brain through my eyes. The birds were brainless; all energy. I grabbed the mirror and held it upright; I caught a half-glimpse, from the tail of my eye, of the weird lightnings coiled inside it, but even that glimpse coiled my stomach in nervous knots. Shielding my face, I held it upward. The birds flew toward it like a moth to the candle. Shock after shock flowed along my arm. Three more of the horrible falcons fell limp, lifeless—drained.

A strange exhilaration began to buoy me up. The force from the birds was not electricity but a kindred force, which my nerves drank greedily. I thrust the mirror out; was rewarded again by the surge of power, and again the birds, this time by dozens, flapped and fell.

Then, as if whatever had loosed the army of falcons had realized their uselessness, the whole remaining force of the birds wheeled and fled, winging swiftly over the land to the distant donjon that rose high and far into the black midnight.

Recalled—to the Dreamer's Keep!

THE LAST SACRIFICE

The flow of strength had renewed me; I felt that I could face whatever came. I thrust Evarin's mirror into my pocket; flung a word to Narayan and we were riding again, Gamine racing behind us. The blue shroudings had been torn to ribbons by the snappings of falcon-claws; I could see the pallid gleam of naked flesh through the torn veils. The noise of battle behind us grew more distinct; I could make out the explosions and the distant flashes of colored flame. I shuddered; even now that frightful army of falcons might be winging to join Adric and Evarin. The rebels could kill some of them, but for every falcon dead there would be twenty more slaves for Narabedla! What could Narayan's men with their scythes and pitchforks and rude rusty guns do against the incredible science of a Toymaker? Narayan's strained face was ghastly in the moonlight; I needed no telepathy to read his thoughts. Slaughter for his men—what for his sister? Our horses seemed to lag, to drag through a mire of motionless, yet they were at the full gallop of their endurance. The sound of fighting grew closer. Everything in me cried out that I was an utter fool, riding full tilt into a battle in which I had no stake. Yet something else told me, coldly and with a grim truth, that all I possessed was what I might win today, for this was the only world I would ever know; that I would never see my own world again.

Never! And Adric should rot in a hell of his own choosing for that!

The sounds of fighting seemed very close. Narayan pulled up his horse so quickly that it nearly sent Gamine plunging into his back. He said in a low, concentrated voice "Adric isn't at the battle! This way—quick!" He whirled the horse and dashed down a side road at right angles to the way we had been riding. If we had raced before, now our horses seemed to fly. The battle raged behind us; I heard dim screams, the neighing of wounded horses, the muffled sound of earth flying upward, exploded in fire. But it had a dreamy unreal quality, like noises through a nightmare. We had left the forest and were riding across a dark and hummocky plain. Moss padded our hoof-noises; now and then some small furry thing skittered across the track we were following and twice my horse shied at swooping birds and my heart stopped until I saw they were not the falcons of Evarin.

Stark and black against a treeless horizon I could see the Dreamer's Keep, between the small crescents of the two lesser moons. The largest one rode a golden orbit over my head. I rode hunched in the saddle, my eyes on the vast cairn only a few miles away.

Suddenly a vast arch of lightning spanned the sky above the Dreamer's Keep. Blue lightning. I heard Narayan groan like a man in his death-agony. Twisting in my saddle, I saw brooding horror on his face—mingled with pain—and a terrified satisfaction. "The sacrifice—I still—feel it," he breathed in labored gasps, "I still— take from it—Mike! Mike—" His voice held unbearable torture, and the veins in the fair face stood out, black and congested with effort. "If I start to work for—them— promise—promise to shoot me—"

"Oh God—" I gasped.

"Mike, promise! Gamine!"

Gamine spurred the horse to his side; I heard the low voice, sweet, almost crooning. Again the vast arch of blueness spanned the sky. Narayan dug spurs savagely into the side of his horse and raced ahead of us. On the plain, limned starkly against the sky, a horseman appeared. He rode low in the saddle, his horse carrying a double burden, but racing fleetly—to the Keep of the Dreamers. I cursed—I knew that lean crouched figure, knew it as well as my own! Adric rode to the sacrifice—and before him, limp across his saddle, he bore Cynara!

The rest of that nightmare ride is a blank in my mind. The next thing I remember clearly is reining up beneath the lee of the gaunt pile of rocks-on-rocks that was the Dreamer's Keep. There was no sign of Adric or Cynara, no sign of any living person, nothing but the incandescent blue lightning that rayed out now every four seconds or so; Narayan's face was a white death-mask, and Gamine's breathing came in short sobbing pants. I alone was free from the effect. My body throbbed and tingled with the weird energy set free in the night. We flung ourselves from our horses. Gamine tugged futilely at the torn veilings to conceal her face, and for the first time the blurred invisibility wavered and I caught a glimpse of one blue eye, blue as the sky lightnings that rose and flared and died.

The lee of the tower dwarfed us with its massive bulk. Gamine clutched my arm, the cruel fingers digging bruisingly into my flesh. "Listen!"

I strained my ears. All I could hear was a low, not unpleasant humming, like the singing drone of great bees or high-tension wires; but the sound struck both aliens with horror. Narayan opened his lips—

I dug frantically in my other pocket; brought out the Toy Rhys had given me. At sight of it Narayan's haggard face relaxed a little. He caught it from me with quick hands. "Free of Adric—" he breathed with that swift erasure of tension I had seen before. He drew a long, moaning sigh. He closed his eyes for a moment.

Somewhere above us a scream rang out; a cry bestial in its mad appeal. It broke the static immobility that held us, and Narayan, sliding the Toy inside his shirt, turned and began to run around the Tower, Gamine and I panting at his heels.

We came around the corner beneath an arching outcrop of stonework. No one needed to give orders; as one, we scrambled up on the ledge, crowding close together.

I gripped my hand on the knife in my belt. It had a comforting feel. I needed that.

A framed archway let us look down into the inside of the Keep. Below us a voice cried out despairingly—unbelievingly. "Adric—" we heard Cynara cry out, "Adric, no—oh, no—" Under our combined weight the glass shattered; we hurled inward. We found ourselves standing on a great shelf, about ten feet above the interior floor of the Keep, looking down at a scene framed in stark horror. Golden Karamy, dwarfed Idris, Evarin—stood in a close circle about a ring of coffins which gleamed crystal—glowed with scintillant radiance. In the hand of each of them was a tiny, jewelled, faceted Toy, and in the coffins—

Gamine screamed.

"The Dreamers—"

Not till then did we see Adric and what he was doing. In the center of the ring of coffins a dais rose upright, horribly altar-like, and a line of the mindless slaves, nude, vacant-eyed, defiled before the altar. As each slave stepped forward there was a shuddering moan from the others, the tiny swords rose and fell and in a brilliant flame of blue light, the slave—was not! And Adric—Cynara struggling between his hands—was thrusting her forward, into the space between the coffins, toward the nexus of the blue light—toward the Sacrifice-stone of the Dreamers!

The sight put us beyond caution. We threw ourselves from the ledge—and went down into a writhing, sprawling mass of living flesh. A barked command from Idris, and the slaves swarmed on us, drowning us in smothering bodies. I kicked and sprawled and thrashed and scratched and bit my way to the top of the heap and somehow for a second, I rolled free. That instant was enough. I was on my feet, the knife in my hand. Dragging bodies clung at my heels; I kicked out savagely, felt my boot strike naked flesh, felt and heard the pulpy sound of a skull crushing under the impact of my heel. The sound rocked my stomach, but I was not in a position to be fastidious. My eyes were swimming in trickling blood. Gamine clawed and thrust free and together we elbowed out of the press.

Evarin sprang at me. I thrust blindly with the knife in my hand, ripped into his shoulder, missing the throat by inches. I caught the Toy from his hand as it fell free. A moment of the clinging, tearing melee—then we three—Gamine and Narayan and I were standing back to back in the centre of the ring of coffins. There was a long howl of pain and terror from Evarin and the four Narabedlans flung themselves backward in a panic terror. For within the coffins the Dreamers were waking!

But Adric was no coward. He threw himself quickly forward—caught at Cynara again, and with all the force in his lean arms he flung her—straight toward the nexus of blue light! Narayan and Gamine stood frozen, bound by the Toys in their hands against the light, but I broke free—I passed straight across the cone of blue lightning—

Unharmed! The blasting energy tingled pleasantly in my body as I caught Cynara in mid-air and reeled away from the force that would have meant annihilation for her. Narayan broke away from the paralysis momentarily and caught Cynara's staggering body from my arms. Then I felt the impact as Adric's tall, heavy body crashed against me, felt the shock as my fist smashed against his jaw and heard him grunt as we locked into a clinch that carried us nearer—and nearer to that center of blue energy. A moment we swayed there, at the very edge of the lightning— then Evarin's tensed cat-body hit in the centre of my back—

Again the heat thrust needles through me. Adric was flung clear, but there was an arch of blue that spanned the vault, a wild scream like the death-cry of a panther, and the Toy-maker was—

Gone!

Within the coffins the blue lights wakened, as if the last flare of energy had freed them. Quickly Idris and Karamy ran forward, quickly Adric leaped to join them, thrusting the Talisman Toys against the very lids of the coffins—but too late. The Toys in the hands of Narayan and Gamine spat glaring blue fire, and step by step the Narabedlans retreated; farther,

farther, farther— The coffins were suddenly empty. As if by magic, three old men and a woman of surpassing beauty materialized about Narayan and Gamine. In their faces I could distinguish a curious likeness to Narayan and to old Rhys—and Narayan, within the circle of the Dreamers, reached out and flung the tattered veils from Gamine. A triumphant chant rushed sweetly from the lips of the spell-singer as the veils came away and in the center of the mutants stood Gamine the Dreamer, dwarfing them all by a pure majesty; the majesty of a Dreamer who had never slept! A woman she was, slender and fair and very beautiful and as like to Narayan as a twin sister, and I thought of Isis and the young Osiris as the blue eyes blazed out and the lovely body arched upward in tall freedom from the shrouding veils. Blue lightning swirled and faded and the Dreamer's tower was bathed in trembling iridescent rainbows. Karamy and Idris retreated step by step, slinking back into the shadows. Only Adric stood his ground.

The Rainbows died. The air was void and empty of energy. The Dreamers stood looking on the crouching Karamy with her hidden face, on the bent, gnarled dwarf, on Cynara, kneeling white and radiant, on Adric, who stood with his lips parted, staring at Gamine like a man released from a spell. It was Gamine who spoke, her eyes resting on Karamy.

"She has done much evil." The others clamored, but Gamine shook her head, long pale hair lifting electrically around her face. "No," she disclaimed softly. "Why should they die? They are only an old dwarf—a silly fool who could not make up his own mind—" her eyes dwelt disquietingly on Adric. "And Karamy. They have no power, now we are freed. Pity them—now we are freed."

Adric, slowly, drew himself upright. His slackly-parted lips set firmly and he looked at Narayan with a dispassionate, stubborn shrug. "Kill me, if you like."

"No, Gamine." Narayan stepped toward the man in crimson, "Adric," he said in a strange, half-choked excitement, "I want to see what you saw before—to see what sent you away—to see the thing that drove you mad. Gamine's veils—Gamine, let him see! Show him, Gamine! Show him what he saw then!"

Gamine came forward slowly to where Karamy knelt. "Stand up!" Slowly Karamy rose to her feet. There was no hope in her eyes; no mercy in Gamine's. The two pairs of eyes, cat-yellow and blue, fought for a moment;

it was Karamy's that fell. The Dreamer woman smiled faintly. "My brothers and my sisters," she said at last, "Karamy is beautiful, is she not?"

I suppose no woman on earth has ever been or ever will be as beautiful as Karamy the Golden. She stood proudly, turning to Adric, and I saw longing and love break forth in the man's eyes. He gazed and gazed, and Karamy laughed and held out her arms, and Adric, bemused, went toward her—

"Hold him," commanded Narayan tersely.

One of the Dreamers made a curious sign with his left hand and Adric was arrested; stood gripped in a vise of invisible force.

"See?" Gamine said in a ringing voice, "But now see Karamy—shorn of the Illusion her Dreamer threw! See the form of Karamy that she made me wear! This!" She reached out and touched Karamy with the little Talisman she held.

There was a gasp of horror from many throats. Karamy—Karamy the Golden—there are no words for the change that took place before our eyes. I was sick and retching with horror before the metamorphosis was half complete, and turned away my eyes; Cynara was sobbing softly into her skirt; but Adric, frozen, could not look away.

Gamine's laugh—low and sweet and doubly deadly for its sweetness—reached my ears. "Shall I lend you my veils—sister?" She murmured, mocking, and again the horrible laugh. "NO? Go *forth!*" Her voice was a lashing whip, and with a broken wail, the thing that had been Karamy threw up an arm across the staring sockets and fled away into the night. And we never saw it again.

So that was the end of Karamy the Golden—the end—

A little later I found that Adric and I were staring stupidly at one another, puzzled, but without animosity. Cynara came and slipped an arm round Adric, and I turned away, embarrassed, for the man was sobbing like a child. I was amazed and sick with the enormity of all that I had seen and done. I stood and shivered and shook with deadly chill. I suppose it was reaction.

"Steady!" Narayan's steely hand on my shoulder kept me once again from making an ass of myself. "You've done us a big favor," he said after a few minutes. "I wish I had some adequate way of thanking you—not for myself—for millions of people. Perhaps one day we'll find a way of sending you back to your own world, but—" his shoulders moved negatively, "I can't say—"

Adric's lean non-human face peered over Narayan's shoulder. He looked subdued, and spoke with a curious humility. He sounded sane. "There will be a way, some day. It will take time to find it, now, but—there will be."

Spontaneously we grinned at each other. I could not hate this man. I knew him too well. I knew, suddenly, that we would be friends. Which, indeed, is what happened.

Narayan looked from one to the other of us, troubled; then Gamine's intent face was at his elbow.

"I'll see to these men," she said quietly. "Narayan, they need you, and it's your responsibility. They have to be told why they were wakened, and how; there are slaves to be freed, armies—"

Narayan glanced guiltily over his shoulder at the other Dreamers who stood huddled together in a bewildered little knot. "That's so," he acknowledged gravely, and went to his people. I watched him, feeling as if my one friend here had deserted me; but it had to be that way. Narayan was not our kind. He was the sort of man who could remodel a world; but the look he sent us over his shoulder told Adric and I that we should, if we liked, have a share in that work.

"Now Mike Kenscott," said Gamine, "I want to talk to you."

We left Adric and Cynara in that place, and I cast a wistful glance back at them. Cynara was lovely, and very human, and I suppose I had hoped that in some way she would compensate for my enforced stay in this world. But there was Adric—

Gamine and I stood on the steps of the Dreamer's Keep, and her voice, soft and wistful, mourned in the grey dawn. "No one ever knew I had the Dreamer powers— except old Rhys. Rhys and I were bound together—he knew, and kept me close to him, hid me and helped me. One day Adric found out. It—changed Adric. He—we freed Narayan together. Then Karamy made me what I was—what you saw. It hurt Adric—hurt something in him. I could have cured him, in time, but Karamy had him bewitched. She stripped him of power, of memory. I do not know, but perhaps some day, Adric may remember that I was—I was—"

"Gamine! Gamine!" Adric's voice cried from within, and the next moment he rushed forth—caught the Dreamer woman in his arms, and his mouth met hers and she stood swaying in his arms, laughing and crying together. Cynara, following slowly, smiled with gentle satisfaction. I said, stunned, "What—"

Over Adric's shoulder Gamine's blue eyes met mine in liquid satisfaction and she finished her interrupted sentence. "I was Adric's wife," she said, gently. Cynara's voice was tenderly humorous as we left them together in the glory of the rising sun. "Poor Gamine," she said, "and poor Adric, too. I was sorry for them both. But I wish these men would make up their minds!"

I had an idea.

"Adric's made up his mind," I said, turning my head a little toward the couple who stood, clasped, as if they could never let go. "I suppose—" I came a little closer to Cynara, who stood looking up at me with wide, innocent eyes and lips ingenuously parted, "I suppose that gives me the right to make up my mind. Doesn't it?" She smiled. "Does it?" But her bright eyes had given me my answer, and I never had to make up my mind again.